LAINIE REMEMBERS

Connie
Cassell

iUniverse, Inc.
Bloomington

Lainie Remembers

iUniverse books may be ordered through booksellers or by contacting:

iUniverse
1663 Liberty Drive
Bloomington, IN 47403
www.iuniverse.com
1-800-Authors (1-800-288-4677)

Because of the dynamic nature of the Internet, any Web addresses or links
contained in this book may have changed since publication and may no longer be
valid. The views expressed in this work are solely those of the author and do not
necessarily reflect the views of the publisher, and the publisher hereby disclaims
any responsibility for them.

ISBN: 978-1-4502-5956-9 (pbk)
ISBN: 978-1-4502-5957-6 (ebk)

Printed in the United States of America

iUniverse rev. date: 12/23/10

— Chapter 1 —

I can still remember that day like it was yesterday, but it has been twelve years now since I was taken.

The day was a sunny day in April, and school was out for Spring Break. We didn't have any extra money to go away like some of my friends, so I decided to make the best out of what I could do at and around home.

Mom was working in the yard planting more flowers, and a new tree. She loved watching the flowers and trees grow, and bloom all summer long and into the fall.

I ask her if I could go to the park to play with some friends of mine. I was eight years old, and thought I was a big girl, and could take care of myself. First mom said no, but I told her Joanie and Jill were going to be there too. So she let me go.

My name is Lainie Marie. Mom named me after both of my grandmas. I have always thought that was really neat. Mom finally said I could go to the park, but to make sure I was back home by 3:00 PM. I had my watch on so I would know when to come home.

The park was two blocks from my house, so I started walking. I am always careful to watch for cars when I cross the street.

I made it to the park and there was Joanie and Jill already playing. We all went to the swings first, and then to the pond. We were having so much fun together, but Joanie looked at her watch, and said, Jill , we have to home. Mom told us to be home by 2:00PM.

We all said goodbye, and I decided to play by myself until it was time to go home. I went back to the swings and was not paying any attention to the man in a blue van who pulled into the parking lot near the swing set. I didn't know he had gotten out of the van and was walking my way. All of a sudden he jerked the swing to a stop, put his hand over my mouth, and started walking back to his van. I was so scared, and tried to scream, and kick at, but his hand was so tight over my mouth, I couldn't let any screams out. He told me to calm down, that he wasn't going to hurt me.

There was no one else in the park but me, so no one saw this man grab me. He hurried to the van, jerked open the side door and put me inside and fastened my seatbelt. He gave me a shot of some kind, and I was out. That was the last thing I remember, until I woke up in a room with a couch and a stove and sink in it. To the one side was a chair, and some other furniture. He was sitting in the chair when I woke up.

I just looked at him for a while. He seemed like a nice man, but I thought if he was nice, then he never would have taken me. His hair was blond, like mine, and he had the same color blue eyes as mine. His hair was long and he had it back in a pony tail. He wore a red baseball cap with big letter R on the front.

When he spoke to me, he told me I had to do what he told me to do, and we would get along just fine. He said he wasn't going to hurt me, so I didn't have to be afraid. I told him I was scared, and wanted to go home to my mom. I looked down at my arm where my watch was suppose to be, but it was not on my arm. I thought I must have lost it somewhere, but didn't know where it was at. I was mad at myself for losing it because now I wouldn't know what time it was, and I knew mom would be mad at me for losing it.

The man told me I wasn't going to go home, that I was going to stay with him. He told me my mom had sent him to get me, and told him to keep me with him. He said she was moving and didn't want me with her anymore. I wondered why she would want to move when she just planted flowers, and trees. So I lay on the couch and cried until he came and sat down beside me and held me. He told me everything was going to be just fine.

— Chapter 2 —

At home, mom, Leslie, was looking at the clock on the wall, and it was already 3:30, and Lainie was not back from the park yet. She was beginning to worry, and she got on the phone and called Sheila, Joanie and Jill's mom to see if maybe Lainie had gone over to there house.

Sheila said that Joanie and Jill were both home and had been since around 2:00, but that Lainie was still playing when the girls left the park.

Leslie was now getting worried, so she went to the park to find Lainie. When she got there, the place was deserted, and no one was in sight, that she could see. Of course she couldn't see around the pond.

She called Sheila back on her cell phone, and she ask where all the girls had played, and Sheila told her what her girls had said. They played on the swings and then walked around the pond, then came back to the swings, then it was time for them to come home, and that is where they last saw Lainie.

When she came back up to the swings, she happened to look down at the ground, and her heart nearly jumped out of her chest. On the ground lay Lainies watch, and she knew something had happened, because Lainie would never take it off her wrist. She wanted to pick it up, but knew she shouldn't.

She got on her cell phone and called to police department. She told them she found her daughters watch on the ground by the swings, and her daughter was no where around. She told them her daughter would never take the watch off, but just to bathe.

The police sent an officer to the park. When the officer got there, he started looking around and found a large foot print in the dirt near the swing set beside where the watch was laying.

About that time, an elderly man came walking there way from the pond area. He was carrying a fishing pole. The officer ask him how long he had been there and the man said his name was Larry and that he had been fishing since around 1:30. He said he came here fishing about everyday, just to have something to do. He said he enjoyed being outdoors, and had seen the girls playing on the swings, then two of them left, and just the one girl was all that was left here playing.

He said the girl was swinging when her dad came to pick her up. He said the man had the same blond hair as the girl had. Larry told them the man carried the girl to his van, and they drove away. He told them the van was blue. He said the man had on a red ball cap with a big R on the front. I don't see as good as I use to, but the "R" was pretty good size.

When the police told Larry what really was happening, he became very upset. Leslie was crying now, and she was blaming herself for letting Lainie go to the park by herself.

The officer got busy trying to find more evidence in the park, so maybe they could find the person who took Lainie. He started walking towards the parking spaces, where Larry had pointed the van had been sitting.

When he got to the edge of the lot, he found a hair barrette laying in the grass at the edge of the lot. He ask

Leslie if it was Lainies and she said that it was. Said she had two of the in her hair that day, but just one was found.

The officer called in more officers and even called for the canine unit to come too to try to help. He told Leslie they need something with Lainie's scent on it, so she went home to get something, and was back by the time the canine unit got there.

The dogs got her scent, and went around the park in all the places Lainie had been playing, and then came back to the swings where they started barking and stopped where her watch was still laying, and then the dogs headed straight to the parking lot where the van was parked earlier. They headed out of the lot and started to turn left, and so the officers knew that the van had turned left, headed east, out of the lot, but that was all the dogs could do. The officers would have to find other ways to try to fine Lainie now.

— Chapter 3 —

Lainie was getting hungry, so she told the man she wanted something to eat.. He said please, call me Ian, and he got up and opened a cooler, which she hadn't seen before, and pulled out sandwiches and two cans of pop. He ask her if she wanted some chips to go along with her sandwich, and she said yes,.

She ate every bite and drank the pop. She needed to go to the bathroom, but didn't see one. She told Ian what she had to do, and he told her the bathroom was outside. He lead her outside and she saw a small house with a moon shape on the door, The Ian told her it was an outhouse. She looked around her and found they were out in the woods.

The woods around her were very pretty. She saw a stream off to the right of the cabin, and mountains that were off behind the stream. The trees were all pine trees. The side of the cabin was piled high with sawed and split wood.

I saw his van parked a ways back into the trees. He told me to go ahead and use the outhouse, and that he would get us some water from the stream to wash with. He went back into the cabin and got a bucket and headed to the stream I went into the outhouse, and by the time I came back out, he was back with the water. When we went back into the cabin, I looked around and was surprised to find several rooms that I had not noticed before.

I guess I was just to scared to see anything, but now that I knew Ian wasn't going hurt me, I looked more.

Ian spoke to me and ask how I liked my new home. I told him I wanted to go back to my mom, but he said that my mom had told him that I was to live with him from now on. He said she had moved to another town and couldn't take me with her.

Of course, started to cry again because I missed my mom. He came to me again and put his arms around me, and told me that everything would be just fine, that I would love living here with him.

She told him her name was Lainie, and he said he knew that, and told me I was a pretty little girl, and that he would take good care of me.

We ate lunch and Ian ask if I would like to go for a walk, and see how beautiful the area was that they were staying in. He said the cabin was built by his grandpa years ago, and now it was his, since his grandparents were both gone now.

We walked along the stream a while and I was surprise when I saw the fish that were jumping in the water. Ian told me we could go fishing later if I wanted to. We continues walking, and I could see some flowers blooming near the base of the mountain. They made me think about the flowers mom was planting in the yard that day. I missed her so much, but Ian had reassured me that mom wanted me to stay with him.

We headed back to the cabin when the sun started going down. Ian grabbed two fishing poles, and we walked over to the stream. We had no more than threw our lines into the water, when both of us caught a fish. After we both caught three each, we headed back to the cabin. Ian showed me how to clean the fish, then he fried them up for our dinner. They were really good, and just the thought of catching them ourselves made it even better.

Night time had come, and I was tired from all the walking, so Ian pulled down a ladder from what he called a loft. He gave me one of his old t-shirts to sleep in. I climbed up the ladder and saw a small bed up there that had a pretty pink cover on it. He told me goodnight, and I crawled into the bed and was asleep in no time at all.

I woke up the next morning when the sun was shinning thru the window by the bed. The window had pin curtains up to it too just the same as the cover on the bed. I crawled out of bed and down the ladder. I told Ian that I was going out to the outhouse, and would be right back.

Ian said he would fix us some breakfast, and then after we ate, we were going in town to buy me some clothes. He said after all, you can't wear the same clothes all the time.

I thought I might be seeing some of my friends while I was there. We got into the van and he told me to fasten my seatbelt, and off we went. I tried to look to see where we were, but nothing looked familiar to me at all. There were lots of mountains all around us.

I ask Ian if we were going to Allenville, and he said honey, we are now where near there right now. I ask him where we were, because I had never seen mountain near where mom and I had lived.

He told me we were in the state of Colorado. I kind of remembered that on our maps at school that it was a long way from Ohio.

We drove for what seemed like an hour, and finally came into a big town. Ian drove to a Walmart Store, and we got out and went in. We got a cart and went to the girls clothing section. Ian picked out several pairs of jeans, and some shorts and tops. He got me a pretty blue jacket then some socks, shoes and underwear, and a bathing suit. Next we went to the hair products where he got me a hair brush and comb and some things for my hair.

We bought food to take back with us and by the time we got to the register, the cart was full. The total amount came to over $270.00. I thought that was a lot of money to spend, but Ian told me not to worry, that I was a pretty little girl and I had to look pretty.

We also stopped at McDonalds for lunch before heading back to the cabin. I loved eating at McDonalds. Mom and I use to go there about once a week for lunch.

When we got back to the cabin,

I helped Ian take everything in. He told me to put my clothes up in the loft in the dresser and there was a small closet to hang what I could hang up. The loft was pretty good size. It ran half the length of the cabin. Ian had a bedroom downstairs off the living room. He had books in a large bookcase, and I went to see what kind of books they were. He told me he was going to be my teacher here at the cabin. There were all kinds of school books, like the ones I had in my class at school.

We sat down and started my first lesson that afternoon. Ian told me since we lived so far from town that his teaching me here was the best. I didn't realize until later years that he didn't want anyone seeing me and knowing who I was.

The years seem to fly by and I was growing into a woman. Ian would let me drive his van some when I turned sixteen, but just around the area of the cabin. When we went into town, he stayed right with me all the time. He never let me out of his sight.

— Chapter 4 —

The police never stopped looking for Lainie. They followed every lead they had, but she seemed to have vanished off the face of the earth.

Leslie always thought each day about Lainie, and wondered if she were dead or alive. She never gave up hope of one day finding her little girl again. It has been eight years, and she thinks and wonders what Lainie would look like now. Would she still have her long blonde hair, or would she have it cut short, and dyed a darker color. Would she have a boyfriend who takes her to the movies and dances.

The worries and wonders seem to take there toll on Leslie. Two years after Lainie was taken, Leslie met Jason Stillings, and they got married and had a son they named Jay, and then a daughter they named Laura. Leslie often thought that Lainie would love her brother and sister, because she had always wanted other siblings in the family.

Leslie thinks now that Lainie would be sixteen years old and a woman, then the tears fell down her checks. She still remembers that day, and feels the anger she had then to find out Lainie was missing.

Where are you Lainie. Are you alive or are you dead. What kind of a monster would steal you away from me. These are questions that one could ever answer for her. 'it was something she had learned to live with.

Leslie's mom came to stay with her after Lainie was taken. Leslie was a basket case, and she had to be kept sedated for a while. She felt like she was going around in a fog all the time.

All the question, about who she thought might have taken her little girl. Did she have any trouble with anyone, did she think Lainies dad had anything to do with this? She told them Lainies dad had died when Lainie was just three years old from a wreck. The truck she told them went off a mountain road out west in an ice storm, and it was burnt so badly that the body was nothing but ashes.

Leslie's life was good now with Jason, Jay and Laura. They had settles down in a small town in Tennessee. She was extra careful with the kids and she would not let Laura go anywhere without adult supervision. She was taking no chances on someone grabbing her. She thought if only I had been that careful with Lainie, she would still be here with me.

She still kept Lainies pictures sitting around on the mantel over the fireplace. Jason told her she would never forget Lainie, and he would support her in any way he could, in trying to find out where she was. He said even though I didn't know Lainie, he still thought of her as his own too.

On the day that Lainie would have turned eighteen, Leslie and Jason added another little girl to there family. They both talked about it and had decided to name her Lane Marie after Lainie. She had the same blond hair and blue eyes just like Lainie when she was borne. Closer inspection of her little body, showed the same birthmark of a strawberry exactly like Lainie had and even in the same place on her right shoulder.

When Leslie saw that she cried, and told Jason it was like she was given a second chance to make things right. Little Lane Marie was growing so fast and at two years old, she was the spitting image of her sister, who now was twenty years old. Lane had the same way of talking and doing things that Lainie had at that age.

— Chapter 5 —

When Lainie woke that morning, she was so happy. Ian had told her he was taking her out to dinner to celebrate her eighteenth birthday. She dressed up really nice in her blue sundress and had her hair brushed and ready to go even before Ian was ready. Her blonde hair fell below her waist, and when he looked at her, he was so proud. He knew he had done the right thing by taking her all those years ago.

Staying in the cabin his grandfather had built was the best thing he knew to do, and just going into town only when he needed to. His van had long ago quit running, and he had bought a 4 wheel Jeep to drive.

There was no newspapers around to read, so Lainie never knew that anyone was looking for her. He didn't want anyone to know he had her. He treated her very well and she liked him, and she never questioned her again about her mom. She thought of Ian as her dad now.

She thought about her mom lots of times, but she had resigned to the facts that her mom had given her away to Ian.

Ian knew that one day soon, he would have to sit her down and tell her everything, but now wasn't the time to do that.

They drove into town and ate dinner at a nice steak house, and he even bought her a birthday cake. While they were eating, he pulled a box out of his pocket, and handed it to Lainie and said Happy Birthday to my girl. She took the box and opened it, and inside was a necklace with a locket on it. She opened the locket and inside was two pictures. They were of an older man and woman. Lainie looked at Ian and ask her who the pictures were.

Ian only smiled and told her on her twenty first birthday, he would reveal the mystery to her. She thanked him for the necklace, and put it around her neck. She told Ian she was going to wear it all the time and not take it off. She said I have a feeling these people here in the locket are going to very special to me. She had three years to wait for she would finally know just who they were.

She loved the locket and would open it and look at the pictures of the man and woman inside often. The photos looked familiar, but she could not remember anthing more than that.

— Chapter 6 —

Leslie was enjoying life with her family, and loved watching the kids grow up. While Jay and Laura were in school, Leslie would take Lane for walks in her stroller and go to the park and swing her on the swings, They would plant flowers in the flower bed, and Lane loved to play in the dirt and try to help. Of course, Lane got more dirt on her than the flowers did, but they had fun.

When they were done, Leslie took Lane inside and gave her a bath, and fed her lunch. While Lane was eating, Leslie grabbed the phone and called the Allenville police department. She always kept in touch with them to see if they had found out any information during the ongoing investigation.

She was surprised when she found out the office who had headed the search had died from a heart attack the month before. They told her another officer had taken over the case, and they would transfer her over to talk to him.

The officer, detective Adam Johnson, told her that the only new he had was that they thought they had found the van that was used, but it turned out not to be the same one at all. So, no, they had nothing more to tell he. Detective

Johnson told her they would keep in touch with her if they heard anything.

Leslie hung up the phone and picked Lane up out of her high chair and layed her down for her nap. She was thinking about Lainie, and somehow she just knew that she was alive somewhere out there. She just had that feeling. It was as if she could feel Lainie close to her.

I was at that same moment in the cabin that Lainie was thinking about her mom. She thought she could feel her mom right there with her. She shivered as a cold chill came across her arms.

Leslie shook the feeling off and went about cleaning her kitchen back up. It seemed weird to her that there were times when she felt Lainie's presence with her. Maybe she thought. Laine is dead, and buried somewhere all alone, and it was her spirit trying to be near me.

— Chapter 7 —

Back at the cabin, Lainie had went fishing with Ian and then they swam. They had caught enough fish for a few days. The water from the stream was cold enough to keep the fish fresh until they ate them.

Lainie had grown into a beautiful young lady. She had all of her schooling done and had her certificate that said she had graduated. She had a straight A average in all her work. She was looking at her maps one day when she told Ian that one day she wanted to go to Rome.

Ian thought enough time had passed since he had taken Lainie, that no one would believe her to still be alive. So as a reward for her, he managed to get a passport for her and one for himself.

The trip was all set up for her twenty first birthday. He told her and she was so excited, she said , we have to go shopping and buy some clothes to take with us. So they went shopping for clothes and other things they would need. She was so excited, but she had no one her own age around to talk to. She just had Ian.

She had started calling him dad now, and had been for a couple of years now.

The day finally came, and they were off to the airport in Denver. They had a lay over in Chicago, then on to Rome. It would be a seven hour flight, but she didn't care one bit, she was going to Rome, Ian loved watching her and was enjoying the fact that she was so happy. This trip would do them both good.

They slept on the plane, so when it landed, they went to there rented villa, and settled in. Since it was still day time outside, they decided to go for a bite to eat. After a short lunch, they went sight seeing. Lainie was so enthralled with Rome. Her schooling had included language courses, so she could speak with all the people there in Rome. Some of the locals told them where to go to see some of the sights that only the locals knew where they were. They had so much fun and walked until they were so tired, but still had fun.

They went to some of the beaches there in Rome, and Lainie was a big hit with all the Italian men. She had a nice tan from all the swimming she had done at the lake hear the cabin. The men couldn't keep there eyes off her.

One young man come up to her and started talking. He was an American there on a vacation, and work too. He told her that he was from Denver, Colorado. That surprised her, and she said that they lived about two hours out of Denver.

He told her his name was Jacob Simmons. For the rest of the trip, Jacob and Lainie were together. The three of them visited museums and art galleries, and went to several eateries. Ian thought Jacob seemed like a very nice man, so it didn't bother him seeing Lainie getting along so well with him.

As time neared to return home, Lainie was sad to have to say goodbye to Jacob. To her surprise, he told her he was ready to go back home too. That his vacation time was over and he had to get back to work .

As fate would have it, he was on the same flight as Lainie and Ian., When they got to the Denver airport, Jacob ask them if they wanted to come to his house and have dinner .

He said he had called ahead to his housekeeper and she was cooking a nice dinner for the three of them.

Ian wanted to say no, but the sheer delight on Lainies face made him agree. He was tired from the flight home, and they still had two hour drive to go to get to the cabin.

At the airport, Ian got his Jeep and he and Lainie followed Jacob to his house. As they were driving, Lainie told Ian she really liked Jacob, and thought he liked her too. Ian told her that he thought she was right.

Jacob signaled and turned into a long winding driveway to his house. When Ian got closer to the house, he was so surprised at the size of the house, he darn near hit Jacob's car in the rear, and would have if Lainie had not yelled at him.

The house looked like something out of a magazine. The law was very nicely landscaped and the house was like none he had every seen before.

Jacob got out of his car and came back to open the door for Lainie, she said, Jacob, do you live here? This is such a beautiful house. He told them to come on in.

His housekeeper, Mrs. Jenson opened the door for them. She told Jacob they all had time to relax and clean up a bit before dinner was ready. Jacob showed them to two separate bedrooms with there own baths. He told them they were welcome to spend the night if they would like since he knew they were tired and had a ways to go to get home.

Ian reluctantly agreed to do that, of course Lainie was thrilled at the thought of having a big four poster, and her own bathroom right there. Jacob told them dinner would be ready by 7:00, and since it was only 3:00, they might want to go out by the pool and maybe swim for a while and relax.

Ian went out to the Jeep to get there bags and brought them in. Lainie changed into her bathing suit, and walked out to the pool area. The pool was so big, and the water looked so blue. She grabbed a towel, and laid it on a chair by the pool and jumped into the clear blue water.

She swam the length of the pool three times and then stepped back out and grabbed the towel to dry off. She was caught up in her swimming that she hadn't noticed that Jacob and Ian had joined her in the pool area.

Jacob ask her if she was enjoying herself, and she told him was very much. She started to walk over to where the men were at and she tripped on her towel. Jacob immediately grabbed her to keep her from falling. While he held her in his arms, he kissed her. He had been wanting to do that again since he kissed her in Rome.

She responded to his kiss to and put her arms around his neck and clung to him, as he deepened the kiss. He finally pulled apart from her, but held her hand and led her to one of the chaise lounges to sit down.

After dinner was over with, Jacob ask if Ian and Lainie would like to watch a movie, but Ian knew they wanted to be alone, so he said he was tired and was going to bed.

Lanine and Jacob had the movie on, but they were doing more kissing than they were watching the movie. They talked about what each wanted out of life, and Jacob told her he really liked her a lot. She told him she liked him too.

When Ian went to his room, his thoughts were on Lainie. He was going to have to tell her soon, but he still had time. There was no hurry yet.

Jacob walked Lainie t o her room and kissed her again before she went inside the room. He told her he didn't want her to leave, but she needed to get her rest, and he would see her in the morning.

The next morning, he met her as she was coming out of the bedroom, and pulled her into his arms and kissed her passionately. He told her he thought about her all night long. She said she thought of him too.

They went to breakfast, and found that Ian had beaten them down to the table and was drinking coffee, and eating eggs and bacon with pancakes and fresh fruit. After they were all done eating, Ian told Lainie they had to get moving and head home. Jacob didn't want to let her go, but didn't argue. He did, however, get directions to the cabin, and told Lainie he would see her real soon.

Jacob knew he had fallen in love with Lainie, and he knew he wanted her for his wife. He had never felt that way about anyone else before.

As Ian and Lainie drove home, he noticed the she was really quiet. He spoke to her in a soft voice, saying, I know that you have strong feeling for Jacob, and things will work out if they are suppose to.

Lainie was thinking about Jacobs kisses, and she wanted more. She thought about his house, and how everything was so nice. It wasn't that she didn't like the cabin, but she would like to have something more. She was no longer a little girl, but a grown woman of twenty one and she was in love.

— Chapter 8 —

Two days after they got to the cabin, she saw a large SUV coming up the lane. She was so excite because of one had ever been there to the cabin since she had came there to live.

When the SUV got close enough, she could see it was Jacob driving it. As soon as he stopped the vehicle, he was out the door running towards her. He pulled her into his arms and kissed her and held her tight, and said he missed her so much and had to come see her.

Ian had been sitting on the porch of the cabin and knew by the looks of it that it would not be long before Jacob took Lainie and married her.

They walked up to the porch and sat down in chairs and started talking to Ian. Jacob told him he loved Lainie, and wanted to ask for her hand in marriage. I know it is old fashioned, but I want to do things right by her. Ian smiled at both of them and said he would give them his blessings.

Jacob pulled out of his pocket a box and opened it. Inside was the most beautiful ring she had ever seen. The diamonds were so large, and it had green emeralds all around the diamonds. Jacob said , this ring was my mothers, and now I want you to have it. She died when I was just sixteen, but gave me the ring just before she died, and told me to give it to my wife one day. That next day, she was gone. She had breast cancer and had fought it for six years. The doctors did all they could do for her. My dad just quit living after mom died, and then when I was eighteen, and while driving his BMW, and fell sleep at the wheel, and I lost him that day too.

It was hard for me with both parents gone, but my grandparents helped me out all they could. They showed me that I could not give up, and that I had to make something of myself, and so I did. I worked hard and got my college degree, and then took over the family business.

Lainie, will you marry me? That was not a hard question for her to answer, and she said "yes", I will marry you..

Jacob invited them back to the house so they could make some wedding plans. He told Lainie he would buy her the most beautiful dress and they would have there wedding there at the house.

With everything packed from the cabin, Lainie rode back with Jacob. Ian told them he wanted to drive back himself so he would have his car there so when he decided to come back to the cabin, he could do so. He had lots of time to think on the long drive back to Jacob's house. What am I going to do, he ask himself, do I tell her, or just leave things the way they are? He worried and fretted the whole trip, but still had no answer for himself when he got there.

The house was in such a happy turmoil with all the planning and preparations that had to be done before the big day. A wedding planner came to talk to them about what they wanted for their wedding.

She was so caught up in all the planning that she didn't notice that Ian didn't seem like himself. She thought it might just be all the hustle and bustle around them.

She finally found a picture of the wedding gown she wanted, and after a seamstress had came to the house, and all the measurements were taken, they picked out the material or the gown, and the seamstress said she would get right on it for her.

Two weeks later the seamstress called and told her she needed to come for a fitting, that she had the gown almost done. The wedding was just two months away, and she was never any happier in all her life.

Jacob was so sweet to her and gave her everything she wanted and lots of time she thought he was spoiling her with all the clothes and jewlery. The one piece of jewlery she would not take off was the locket that Ian had given her on her eighteenth birthday. She still opened it and looked at pictures inside. Ian had told her he would tell her who the people were when she was twenty one, and now she was that age.

She decided to ask Ian now who the people were in the locket, so she went to find him. He was sitting out on the pool deck drinking a glass of iced tea. When he saw her coming towards him, he smiled at her. She sat down beside of him and said, now is the time for you to tell me who these pictures are of.

He said yes it is, honey, these are my mom and dad, and if they were still alive they would love you so very much. They are your grandparents.

— Chapter 9 —

Time was flying so fast, and her wedding was just was just a week away. She hoped the sun would continue to shine . The flowers were blooming so pretty, and she knew they would be next week too.

The day of her wedding , the sun was shinning so bright, and the lawn was blooming with all the colorful flowers everywhere you looked. The pool area looked like something out of a magazine. There were lotus blooms in the pool floating around.

The wedding planner helped me into my gown and the I walked down the isle with Ian at my side. I felt like a princess going to a ball. There were so many people taking pictures, and so many cameras.

I knew Jacob was important in the community, but never realized just how important until my wedding day. He looked so great in his tux. As Ian walked Lainie down the aisle , she thought she was the luckiest girl in the world to be marring the handsomest guy around and to have her dad beside her and she was going to marry the man she loved.

After the minister pronounced them husband and wife, Jacob kissed her. As I turned around I saw tears in Ian's eyes, and then he smiled and blew me a kiss. I know he was happy for me.

— Chapter 10 —

Leslie was getting ready for Lane's birthday party. She was turning six in two weeks. She thought, and yes, Lainie will be twenty two that same day. She still thought about Lainie a lot. Thinking about her when she should have been helping her get ready for proms and dance and graduation.

Now her thoughts were running to the day when Lainie would have been married. Jay and Laura were growing up and soon it would be time for Laura to go to prom and then graduation. She hoped Laura would go to college to become a teacher. She had said that is what she wanted to do.

Jay, on the other hand, just wanted to work with his dad, or have his own farm so he could raise dairy cattle like his grandpa does. He loved going to his grandparents house every chance he could, and help them out. Most weekends and then in the summer that is where he would stay.

Most of the summer, it was just Jason, Laura, Lane and me at home. We would take the girls to the movies, and then go for ice cream. Lane seem to have the same tastes as Lainie did when she was that age.

Leslie thought more about Lainie since it was getting close to the anniversary of when she was taken. Leslie would call the police in Allentown on Monday to see if they had found anything else yet. The weekend passed by and Monday came.

She made her phone call and talked again to the officer who had taken over the case. She ask if they had anything new yet, but was told nothing new had came in in all. She was so discouraged that nothing had ever been found except for Lainie's watch and her hair barrette. I t seemed like she just never existed at all, or just disappeared into thin air.

She has to be somewhere, or in a shallow grave , but nothing was ever found, and no one could find out who took her.

After hanging up the phone, Leslie sat down and cried like she always does. She was wiping her eyes when Lane came into the room. Lane ask her what was wrong, but Leslie told her she was just thinking about another litte girl she knew.

She had never told Lane about Lainie. It was always to painful to talk about with her kids. Still she never stopped thinking about or loving Lainie.

— Chapter 11 —

Jacob and Lainie were getting ready to go on their honeymoon. He was taking her to Hawaii for a month. He thought that it would do her good to get away and enjoy herself again like she did in Rome, but this time she would be his wife..

Ian gave Lainie a big hug and kiss on the cheek and told her he was heading back to the cabin. Jacob ask him if he would stay and help keep Cheryl, his housekeeper company while they were gone. He told Ian. There was plenty of room, and he knew Lainie would want him to be close by.

Ian agreed to stay at the house while they were gone. Jacob told him, he had something he wanted to give to him before he and Lainie left. He took Ian out to the large six car garage. He opened the door and walked in. He turned the lights on and Ian was surprised to see all the cars inside.

Jacob got a set of keys off the hooks by the door and handed them to Ian. It took him by surprise when Jacob told him the blue SUV in the third space now belonged to Ian. He told Ian he knew the Jeep wasn't going to last much longer, and he wanted him to have the SUV as a gift from him and Lainie.

Ian thanked him for the vehicle and told him he was glad Lainie had found someone as nice as he is. Jacob told him he loved Lainie with all his heart, and he would always treat her like a queen , and he would do anything in the world for him too since he was he was her father.

After The happy couple left for there honeymoon, Ian went into the den to see if he could find a good book to read. He walked over to the shelves that were all around the room. He found books on everything imaginable, and lots of novels.

He found ne novel that he thought he would like, and sat down in the big leather chair to read. He had been reading for about two hours when the housekeeper came in and told him his lunch was ready.

He told her he would be right in, and started to lay the book on the ottoman, and it fell off onto the floor. When he reached for it, a piece of newsprint fell out of the book onto the floor. He picked it up and started to read it. The headlines read, "millionaire" dies after falling asleep at the wheel.

Ian read the article. It stated that Mr. Bryce Simmons had dies on impact in the crash. IT also said he had lost his wife two years previously to cancer, and that his intire fortune was left to his son, Jacob.

Ian knew Jacob's parents had both died, but he had never told him or Lainie that he was a millionaire.

That did explain the house and all the vehicles , and all the nice things he had. Even thought Jacob had lots of money, he was just a down to earth person, and Ian was glad that he and Lainie had fallen in love and gotten married. He knew Lainie didn't care about all the money, and just so she was happy was all that mattered. He hoped they had a great time in Hawaii.

When he finally got to the kitchen, Mrs. Jenson had fixed a nice seafood salad and some iced tea. He ask her to join him and talk while they ate. She joined him and they talked about everything. He told her he had found the newspaper atrticle about Jacobs dad, and she said that was such a shame, because Jacobs dad was so nice, and then she added so was his mom.

She told Ian she had to make a trip to the grocery store to pick up some things for the house, so he ask if she would like a ride, and she accepted because she really liked Ian.

He ask her if she would like to go out to dinner tonight, and she said she would love to. That night they went to a nice Italian restaurant, then they went to a movie. When they returned to the house, Ian gave Cheryl a kiss.

She told him her husband had died three years ago, and the at times she got so lonely. He told Cheryl that he had been married when he as very young, but had been alone now for a long time except for Lainie. He told her he was getting older and would like to find a nice woman, like herself to be with.

They talked long into the night, and then went to there bedrooms. Ian gave her another goodnight kiss, and told her he would see her in the morning, and that he woud make breakfast for her this time.

— Chapter 12 —

Jacob and Lainie were having a great time in Hawaii. They lay on the beach, and swam. They took long walks don the beach and night strolls. She was getting so tanned, and her skin just glowed. They spent lots of time in bed making love to each other. She often wondered how she was so lucky to have found such a wonderful man .

There third week there, Lainie got up and when she smelled the food room service had brought, she headed for the bathroom. She told Jacob she thought she had caught the flu, or maybe it was just all the excitement, but she just wasn't feeling very well. This went on for several days, and then je said he was going to get a doctor to look at her.

The doctor arrived in less than an hour, and went into the bedroom where Lainie was laying down. He ask her lots of questions and then ask her when her last period was. She told him it had been over a month, and that she was late, but just figured it was just nerves that caused her to be late. He ask her to come into his office so he could run some tests to make sure, so she told him she would be in the office that afternoon.

At the doctors office, the tests were ran, and she and Jacob were sitting in the exam room when the doctor came back in, He was smiling, and then he said "congratulation", you are going to have a baby. From what I can tell you, the baby will be born around January of next year.

The doctor told her at least now she knew it wasn't the flu. He told her she was having morning sickness, and that she might have it for a month or so, but he could give her something to hopefully stop it.

Jacob was so happy that he grabbed Lainie off the exam table and swung her around, and told her he loved her so much, and that now they were going to have a family.

He ask her if she wanted to go back home, and they both agreed it would be the best thing to do. After getting the jet ready to fly back home, and getting everything packed, they headed to the airport.

He told her he was so happy that she was going to have his baby. He then told her, he would like to have four or more children, and she readily agreed. He said that since they were both only children that it will be nice to have our kids grown up with other siblings to play with, and she agreed.

There flight back to Denver was so smooth, and after they landed, and had there luggage, and were in the car headed home. Lainie told Jacob that Ian would be so happy to, now he was going to be a grandpa.

They called and old Ian and Mrs. Preston, who was now just Cheryl to Ian, that they were coming home. But gave no explanations as to why they cut there honey moon short. They wanted to see the looks on there faces when they told them that Lainie was pregnant.

When they pulled into the driveway, both Ian and Cheryl came out to meet them. They were both curious as to why they were home early, but didn't ask any questions.

After they got settled, they told Ian and Cheryl they both wanted to talk to them. Of course, they noticed that Ian and Cheryl had grown close to each other, and they saw the looks that were going on between the two of them. Lainie was happy for them too.

Ian told them he wanted to talk to them too, but his could wait until later. He wanted to hear what was so important that they cut the honeymoon short.

Lainie looked at Jacob, and smiled and then she told Ian he was going to be a grandpa. He could not contain himself, and got up from the chair and gave Lainie a big hug, and told Jacob they had made him the happiest man around.

Cheryl added her congratulations to all of them, and said thing are really going to change around here now that a baby is on the way.

The nursery would have to be redone since it was still the same as it was when Jacob was a baby. It would be so much fun to have a baby in the house again, Cheryl was as anxious as everyone else was.

Cheryl ask Lainie how she was feeling, and she told her about her morning sickness she was having. Cheryl told her she had an old time remedy that might help her with tht, so they both headed off to the kitchen.

When Jacob and Ian were alone, Ian told him that he had found the newspaper clipping about his dad. He told Jacob how sorry he was that his parents couldn't be there to help celebrate the news of a new baby. Jacobs eyes grew misty, and said they are here in thought if not in person. He said his mom would have loved seeing her grandchildren.

He said his dad was always so busy that he never had time for family things, and after mom died, he lost interest in everything. He seemed to die the day mom did. He just didn't want to live without her.

Jacob said he now understand just how his dad felt, because he loved Lainie so much and he didn't know what he would ever do if he lost her. Dad did do a few things with me after mom died, but his heart just wasn't in it. We just had each other and we did the best we could.

Dad and I planted that red oak tree out in the yard as a tribute to mom, then after dad died, I planted the second one in his honor. When the kids get bigger, we can put swings in the tree for them to play on. That will be like mom and dad are there cradling them while they play.

Jacob told Ian that he and Lainie had talked and they both want at least four children. So be prepared grandpa to have several grandkids to play with, and spoil.

Ian told Jacob that he and Cheryl had gotten pretty close while he and Lainie were on there honeymoon. He knew something was up with the looks he saw each of them giving the other, and he told Ian that he was glad, that he gave them both his blessing too. He said Cheryl has had some rough times, but has always pulled through each time, and I am glad she has someone to make her happy.

Lainie and Cheryl came back into the room and they were all smiles, because Cheryl had told Lainie about her and her dad . Lainie gave Ian a hug and said, looks like you had a nice time too while we were gone. She told him she was happy for them and they deserved to be happy , and it was about time he found someone.

Cheryl went to stand beside Ian and he put his arms around her and told Jacob and Lainie that he and Cheryl wanted to get married too if it was alright with them. Jacob nor Lainie had any problems with that at all, they were delighted at the thought of it.

Cheryl said they just wanted a very small wedding, nothing big and she wanted to invite her sister ti come if that was alright with Jacob and Lainie. It was April so they made plans for a June wedding.

Jacob told them they could either live in the big house with them, or they could have the gate house. It was there choice as to where they wanted to live. The gate house was a cute little two bedroom house. That is where they decided to live for now.

Jacob had a crew come in and repaint the inside for them, and told them to pick out new carpet and the furniture they wanted in there too, and that he was paying for it. He said that Cheryl had helped him out so much and had been there for him after his parents died, that he wanted to do something for her.

— Chapter 13 —

Everything was going so great that Ian was afraid something would go wrong, but nothing did. At last June came and just a few days now and Cheryl would be his wife. It had been a long time sine he had a woman, but she made him feel so loved, and he knew he was doing the right thing. He loved her so uch more than he thought he ever could. She was good for him.

The wedding was small and Cheryl's sister, Jill and her brother-in-law Tom, came from Arizona to the ceremony. The was the first time they had been together now for six years. Cheryl was so busy taking care of Jacob, and the house, that she didn't have time to go anywhere.

Cheryl wore a pale blue dress and carried a ring of small yellow tea roses. When Ian put the ring on her finger, a tear fell from her eyes. They had a small reception after the wedding around the pool area.

Jacob and Lainie surprised Ian and Cheryl with a trip to New York for there honeymoon. Cheryl had always wanted to go there, and now it was her chance to go. She thanked Jacob and Lainie and Ian gave her a hug and a kiss, and said well, my wife, looks like we are going to "New York.

Jill and Tom spent that night at the house and they left the next morning to head back to Arizona. They wished Ian and Cheryl the best, and told them to come to see them sometime soon. Cheryl was glad to spend what little time she could with her sister, but knew they had to get back home, because Tom's dad wasn't doing very well.

After they left, Cheryl and Ian started packing so they could leave too. New York was so nice and they had so much fun. They went to theaters and took walks in Central Park, went to the Statute of Liberty and even to Ground Zero where the twin towers had once stood. They had a very nice time, but it was time to go back to Denver again. Cheryl was ever more happy. She had a man she loved and he loved her to. They were starting a new life together They were going to take things one day at a time, and make the most out of what years they had left.

After they returned me, Cheryl still cooked the meals and Lainie was always there to help her out. Lainie was a very good cook and she loved to bake. The kitchen always smelled so good with one of Lainie's desserts in the oven.

Her morning sickness was gone and she felt fine. She was three month along now in her pregnancy and was already beginning to show a little. Jacob was always coming up and patting her stomach, and asking how is my baby. He loved the idea of children so he could spoil them too. He would have to wait until January though before the baby was born.

The ultra sound at the doctors office when Lainie was six month along showed she was having twins. She and Jacob were so surprised by the news , but as the doctor moved the wand over her stomach, he said, what you you think if I told you there is another one in there too. They wanted to know if they were boys or girls or what, so the doctor moved the wand around and then he showed them that there were two girls and one boy. She had never known anyone who had triplets, but she knew they would be a handful. Thank goodness she has Cheryl and Ian there to help her and Jacob out.

Lainie was getting so big with the babies, and the doctor worried about her, but she told him she was just fine.

Summer, and fall flew by and soon it was December, and Lainie wanted a big Christmas tree to decorate, and she wanted the house all decorated up too. Jacob and Ian got a 14 foot tree for the house. They put lights and bulbs on it, but Jacob would not let Lainie climb up the ladder to put the decorations near the top, he said he or Ian would do that.

She had bought so many gifts that were brightly wrapped and already under the tree. She had gotten gift for the triplets too even though they were not here yet. A lot of the gifts were for Ian and Cheryl and for Jacob. On Christmas eve they were sitting around the tree and Lainie had been having some small pains all day, but never told anyone about them, she just thought it was because she had worked so hard the day before.

Jacob noticed her holding her stomach and saw the pain on her face every so often, and he ask her if she was having problems, she told them she was having pains, and now they were coming fifteen minutes apart. So Jacob called the doctor and he told them to meet him at the hospital.

All four of them got into the car and headed to the hospital. By the time they got there her contraction were closer and now they were just five minutes apart. The doctor got there about the same time they did and he immediately had the nurses put her in the delivery room. Five minutes later, she had Ellie, then a minute later, out came Emily and then Ethan.

Jacob , Ian and Cheryl were so amazed at how the babies all had blond hair and the piercing blue eyes like there dad. They were a darker blue than Lainies eyes were.

Jacob took turns with Ian and Cheryl holding each of the babies. This was one of the best Christmas's they had ever had. He was a very proud daddy. Lainie said they are all so beautiful, and then she went to sleep. Ian and Cheryl were equally proud to be new grandparents.

The doctor told them Lainie needed her rest and they could all come back the next morning.

The nursery was all ready, so there wasn't much to do when they got home, so Cheryl packed some clothes for the babies to come home in and little blankets too. She picked out the pink for Emily and Ellie and a blue one for Ethan. She was just as proud as if she were Lainie's mom.

Christmas day was spent at the hospital with Lainie and the babies. All three were sound asleep and woke up only when they wanted something to eat. They never cried, and they smiled a lot. Lainie looked tired, but happy.

The doctor came in and told her she could go home the next morning if everything went ok today with the babies.

The next morning Cheryl helped her dress the babies for there trip home., and Lainie was ready herself. They put the babies in there car seats, and they were on there way home.

With the babies home, the house was always bustling and busy., Ian and Cheryl helped out a lot, and Jacob hired a nurse to help out at the first couple of months so Lainie could get her strength back.

I loved being with my babies, feeding, bathing and rocking the. Jacob was taking just as much interest in the kids and was helping out too. With three rocking chairs in the nursery, and there was always a couple of the in use at all times during the day. Cheryl and Ian were spoiling the babies and would not let them cry. They were the doting grandparents, and glad to help out.

After being home two weeks, all three of the kids were sleeping thru the night, and waking up at 5:00AM for a bottle. One morning while Lainie was feeding Emily, she thought about her mom and was missing her even more, and thinking that her mom was missing out on seeing her grandchildren. Even though Ian had told Lainie so many times that her mom didn't want her and gave her to Ian, she still thought about her.

She didn't want to dwell on that thought, so she started paying attention to Emily and feeding her. She heard Ellie waking up and as soon as she got finished feeding Emily, she went to get Ellie to feed her, then Cheryl came in and she got Ethan and fed him.

The kids grew so fast and they each had there own personalities. They each had that pretty blonde hair and baby blue eyes.

At six months, they were all crawling and teething. Jacob loved taking them out in the yard to sit on a blanket under the Red Oak trees. I walked out to check on them and all three kids were sound asleep and Jacob was staring at them. He told me he felt his mom and dads presents when he had the kids here under the trees She told him she was glad, and wished his mom and dad were still here so they could see there grandkids.

— Chapter 14 —

Leslie was thinking again about Lainie. She could picture how she would look right now and her being married and maybe even having some children of her own. That was just a dream to Leslie though, and she knew it would never come true. She was sure Lainie was dead and buried somewhere and had been for years.

She loved reading magazines and had some that a friend had given her last year that she hadn't gotten around to reading yet. She wanted to get her mind off Lainie, so she picked up the magazine and started reading it. She read several articles in it and when she turned the next page, she started reading the story about a happy couple in Denver who had gotten married and the photos were exquisite,

 It showed the couple, and it showed the gown the young woman was wearing and it was beautiful.

They story said that millionaire Jacob Simmons married at his Colorado home in April, and that he and his new wife were honeymooning in Hawaii.

Leslie looked at the bride and thought she was a very pretty and lucky girl. It said the brides name was Lainie. That made Leslie think again about her Lainie, but didn't think about it too much more.

The story told of Jacobs parents, of his mother dying of cancer when he was sixteen and then losing his dad two years later. It stated that Jacob was left with everything form his parents estate, and was a very wealthy man.

The photos were very good and there were some that showed the happy couple strolling on the beaches in Hawaii.

The next issue she read was a few months later, and again there was an article on Jacob and Lainie Simmons, and it stated that they were expecting triples in January. The picture showed a girl with a very large pregnant belly. Leslie thought it would be nice to have grandbabies, but she thought three might be hard to hands at one time. She knew it would take lots of patients and understanding.

She dug around for the next several issues of the magazine, and it was the January issue, that stated that the triples had come a little early, but all three were doing just fine. She hadn't looked close enough to the photos in the article because she didn't know these people. The only thing that stood out in her mind was the young girls name, that it was the same as her daughters.

Leslie's son Jay had graduated from school and was working with his dad, and Laurie was in her second year of college. Lane was a freshman in high school and she had the long blond hair and the blue eyes just like Lainie had. She was he daddy's girl though. She loved looking at the family albums and one day she found in the bottom of an old dresser in the attic an album she had not seen before.

She started looking through it and saw a girl with blonds hair and she looked like Leslie. Lane took the album downstairs and ask Leslie who the girl in the pictures was. She was sitting on the porch swing and Lane sat down beside her. Mom, she said, I found this album in the old dresser up in the attic and wondered who this girl in the picture is.

Of course Leslie had forgotten about the album, but when she saw the photos of Lainie she began to cry. Lane ask her why she was crying, and Leslie had to explain to her. This is Lainie, she was taken from a park when she was just eight years old, and I have never seen her since. Lainie was my daughter. Lane was speechless, because this was time she had ever heard of this.

Leslie told her that she and Lainie lived in Allenville, Ohio after she dad had died. She told her that Lainie had gone to the park to play with her friends and when time for her to be home, she didn't come back. She told Lane that a witness told the police a man in a blue van had put Lainie in his van and left. The police found her watch and hair barrette near the swings and near the parking lot, but no one ever saw her again.

Oh mom, Lane said, I am so sorry. Now I understand why you would let me go any place by myself. Lane told Leslie she thought Lainie looked like her. Leslie gave her a big hug and kissed her on the cheek.

Lane ask her if she had talked to the police to see if the had found anything, but Leslie told her she hadn't spoken to the officer for a few years now. Leslie told Lane what she thought had happened to Lainie, and she agreed that she might be right, but she hated It that her mom was so hurt by it all.

Leslie told her that she was named after Lainie, and that they had the same middle name, Marie. Lane thought that was nice to be named after a sister she hadn't even known until today that she had. Lane took the photo album in the house, but told Leslie she was going to put it with the rest of them in the den.

— Chapter 15 —

At nine months old the triplets were all pulling themselves up to the coffee table and walking around it. It wouldn't be long and they all three would be walking by themselves.

Cheryl and Ian walked into the room and Ethan looked at them, and let go of the table, and walked over to them, calling nana and papaw. Of course the girls couldn't let Ethan outdo them and they both let go and walked over to them too.

Jacob walked in about that time and the girls spotted him and both walked right over to him, saying dada ,dada. He said to the others , it looks like our kids want to get to where they are going faster. I guess they all have decided that walking is faster than crawling. That afternoon, all three kids were all over the downstairs and into to everything. They didn't want to be picked up now that they knew they could walk, they wanted to be on the go.

Lainie thought Ian looked pale and ask him if he was ok. Cheryl told her that he was tired all the time and seemed to have no appetite any more. Ian told her he had an appointment with the doctor that next afternoon, and for her not to worry. He said you have enough to worry about with these three.

The next afternoon at the doctors office, Ian told doctor about things he had not even told Cheryl about. The doctor told Ian he wanted to put him in the hospital and run some tests on him to see if they could narrow down what might be the problem. He said I have some ideas, but I want to run tests to make sure I am right before I say anything.

Ian agreed to the testing, so the next morning he went to the hospital. He told Cheryl and Lainie and Jacob it was just routine testing, but Cheryl told him she was going with him.

The doctor ran the tests and sent him home. He told Ian to come into the office next week on Wednesday, and he would have his results at that time. Cheryl went in that next Wednesday with him because she was really concerned. When the doctor came into the room, Cheryl knew by the look on his face, the news wasn't good.

Ian, the doctor began, the test results show that you have prostrate cancer, and that it is in the final stages. I am so sorry to have to tell you this, but you have between three to six months to live. If we had caught it sooner, you might have had a chance, but it is to far advanced to do much of anything but keep you as comfortable as we possibly can with medication.

Cheryl broke down at that time, and cried. She ask if there was anything at all that could be done, but the doctor just shook his head, and said if we had found this two years ago, then as I said we might have had the chance to cure him, but it is too far advanced right now, and there is nothing we can do.

The ride home was a somber one. Cheryl ask Ian if he was going to tell Lainie and Jacob. He thought for a while, and then said, yes I have to, she is my daughter and she needs to know. She is strong enough to handle it and she has Jacob and you to lean on.

When they go home, Lainie and Jacob were sitting on the porch swing, and the kids were all three down for there naps. He told thm he had some things he wanted to talk to them about, and it wasn't good news.

He said, I got the test results back and that the doctor told him he had prostate cancer, and that it was too far advanced to do anything about, and that he had three to six months to live. He told all of them he had to get things taken care of before that time. Jacob told him he would help him do what he wanted to do, and for Ian not to worry about Lainie or Cheryl or the kids. Jacob told him he would get an attorney lined up for him to do what he had to do.

A month had passed since that day, and Ian was getting weaker each day. Cheryl was so worried about him, and so was Lainie. Lainie took over most of the cooking so Cheryl could be with Ian most of the time. She was also at Ian's side a lot, and wished she could do something to make him better, but knew there was nothing anyone could do, but be there with him and make him comfortable.

As Ian got weaker, he knew he had to talk to Lainie, and tell her he was her real dad, and that he didn't die in that car crash, that it was a hitchhiker he had picked up that day. He was thrown clear of the car when it went over the cliff.

Ian decided it was time, to he had Cheryl ask Lainie to come to talk to him. She came in and sit down in the chair beside his bed. He told her the whole story. And waited for her to talk. After a few minutes she finally said, so you are my real dad, but I guess I have know that down deep in my heart all these years. You have always treated me like your daughter.

So where is my mom and did she really give me to you? No, Lainie, after your mom thought I died in that crash, Then she got my insurance money, and bought that house in Allenville, Ohio, I didn't want to have to have her give all they money back, so I stayed out of sight. I lost touch with her for a good while, then I looked up on the computer and saw where she was, so one day I drove through Allenville , and I saw you playing in the yard at your house.

I watched you from far away for about a month. I saw you when you waked to that park where I got you that day, and I watched you play with your friends, and then saw them leave to go home.

I missed you so much, and it had been over four years since I had seen you. I wanted you to be with me, so that day after your friends left and you were there by yourself in the park, I decided to take you to Colorado with me to the cabin.

I never though about what your mom would go through when were gone. I only was thinking about myself. I know that was selfish of me, and I thought several times about taking you back, but seemed to adjust so well to life at the cabin, I finally decided I did the right thing. You were happy, weren't you?

Yes dad, I was very happy living with you, but what happened to mom? Ian told Lainie that Leslie had lived two more years in the house in Allenville, then met and married Jason Stillings, and moved to Tennessee.

How do you know all this dad? I always kept tabs on your mom. It wasn't hard to do. I would always check the computers when were went to the library. You were so busy reading things, you didn't notice or pay any attention to what I was doing.

I also read about the police in Allenville not having any clues other than my blue van and that I was wearing a red cap with an "R" on it. They found your watch and hair barrette, but nothing else.

Ian told me I have two sister, ad one brother. Your brother's name is Jay, and your sisters are Laura and Lane Marie. I am sure you will want to get in touch with them, especially your mom. She will be glad to know you have three beautiful children.

I have one request of you though. What is it dad, you know I will do anything for you. Will you please wait until I am gone before you get in touch with the police in Allenville and then your mom? I know I don't have that may days left now.

Lainie had tears rolling down her face, and she said, "yes dad" I will wait. I think I always knew you were my real dad. I remember a little bit when I was little I am glad I had all those years with you.

The next morning, Cheryl called at the house crying, and she told Lainie, your dad wants to see you right away. As Lainie walked into the bedroom, she saw her dad was very pale, and having trouble breathing. He opened his eyes and saw her standing there, and told her he loved her, then smiled, closed his eyes and was gone.

Lainie was so upset and her and Cheryl cried for about half an hour, but Lainie knew she had to pull herself together and get services started for her dad made. Jacob was a big help to her and Cheryl and a support for both of them to lean on.

The services were set up for the second day after her dad died. It was very nice and calming. Cheryl told Lainie she would be there to help her out in anyway she could, she said that Ian would want her to do just that. She told Lainie that Ian loved her so much and he wanted to make things right before he died, and she hoped Lainie was not mad at him for taking her away from her mother.

Cheryl told Lainie that her dad loved the kids and knew that they would miss him too, because he was always playing with them. Lainie said she would make sure the kids always would remember there grandpa.

— Chapter 16 —

The days rolled into weeks, and Lainie finally decided it was time to get in touch with the police and let them know where she had been all those years.

On Monday morning, she called and got the phone number for the Allenville, Ohio police department. She was so nervous about making the call, but she knew that her dad would not be in any trouble, so she made the call.

The officer who answered transferred her to another officer. Lainie told them who she was, and that she was the girl who was taken when she was eight years old form the park there in town. The officer ask her all kinds of question and told her they wanted to send someone out to Colorado to talk to her. They wanted to make sree she was the same girl before they called her mom.

The next day, an officer was at her door. She invited him in, and said his mane was Detective Adam Johnson. When he started talking to her, she told him about her watch that she lost that day, and about the hair barrette too. Detective Johnson knew then that he had the same girl.

He told Laine he was going back to Allenville, Ohio, and that he would put in a call to her mom and let her know that she was alive and well. He told Lainie he would give her mom the phone number and address so she could get in touch with her.

— Chapter 17 —

Leslie was outside working in the flower bed when she heard the phone ringing. She had just got to the house, and the ringing stopped. She wondered who it could have been, and thought if it is important, they will call back.

She saw it was lunchtime, so she washed her hands and was getting something to eat when the phone rang again.

When she answered it, she was surprised to hear the voice on the identy himself as detective Johnson from Allenville police department. Mrs. Stillings, I wanted to call you and Leslie ask f they had found out any new yet.

Detective Johnson ask her if she was sitting down. Then he laughed a little and said yes" we have some news for you. Of course Leslie was thinking the worst, thinking they had found a body and that it was Lainie.

The detective told her that it was really good new. He first started out with the question of her first husband. The detective told her that Ian had not died in that car crash, but had been alive and well living in Colorado all these years. Then he told her that Ian had died about a month ago from cancer.

Now here is the best news though, Lainie was taken that day by her dad and was living with him in a cabin there in Colorado all those years

He told her that Ian had told Lainie the whole story before he died, and how to get in touch with us here at the department, and all about you Mrs. Stillings. He kept tabs on you all these years, so he would know what to tell Lainie when the time came.

Lainie is living in Denver now, I went to talk to her to make sure she was the right girl, and not just someone who was just trying to scam you. She is who she says she is, and she is married to a very nice man and has triplets. I told her I was going to give you her phone number and address, so you could get in touch with her. This is one case

I am glad has a very happy ending. Detective Johnson gave Leslie all the information and said good bye, and good luck to her.

She got off the phone and stared at the information and then sat down and cried. She was so glad to finally find out what had happened to Lainie, and that she was just fine all these years. She thought of all the years she had missed watching Lainie grown up, but was so glad to know she was alive and that she was married, and had children.

Leslie waited until everyone was home for the evening and then she told all her family about the phone call she had gotten that afternoon. She told them the detective told her Lainie had three kids and that she was a grandma and that Ian, her ex husband who she thought was dead all those years had been alive and had taken Lainie that day.

She told the family how Lainie had gotten in touch with the police in Allenville two days ago and they sent someone out to Colorado to talk to her to find out if she was the real girl who had been taken. They were convinced that she was the same girl. She told them how Ian had told her before he died how to get in touch with the police and all about them too.

Leslie said she would call and talk to Lainie tomorrow. Leslie told them that Lainie is married now and has triplets. Jay said now I am an uncle and Laura, an Lane said we are aunts too.

Next day, Leslie waited until noon, Tennessee time to make the call. The phone rang four times, and she was beginning to think no one was home, when suddenly she hear a "hello". Leslie was so stunned she couldn't hardly talk but finally she said she wanted to speak to Lainie . The woman who answered told her that she was speaking to Lainie, Leslie told her who she was, and Lainie said she had been waiting for the call.

Lainie told her about what her dad had told her ,and that they lived in the cabin her grandfather had built.

Leslie told her she remembered that Ian had told her after they were married that his dad had built the cabin there in Colorado, and he was going to take them there when it got warm weather, but of course, that never happened. Leslie said she had forgotten completely about the cabin, until Lainie had mentioned that is where she and Ian had lived all those years.

Lainie told Leslie that Ian was really good to her all those years she was with him. She told her that Ian had taken her to Rome, and that is where she met Jacob.

Lainie ask her if she would like to come to Colorado to her, and her grandkids. Leslie told Lainie that she would love to come out to see her. She told her this is the day she had waited for for many years.

Lainie told her that Ian had said she remarried and that she now has two stepsisters and one step brother. Leslie told her that was right, but how did Ian know all that? Lainie told her dad had kept up on what was going on in Leslies life so when the time came, he could tell Lainie all about it. Why doesn't all the family come out to visit, then I can meet my siblings and get to know each other, while you and I get to know each other all over again. Leslie said that she would love to do just that.

Leslie said she would make the arrangements, and let her know when they were coming, and that she was so anxious to see her again. Lainie also told Leslie how Ian had married Cheryl and what a big help she is with the kids, and that they both missed Ian a lot.

— Chapter 18 —

After Lainie hung up the phone, she sat thinking. Lainie thought it was so amazing that she was going to see her mom again but also scared too. She didn't know if her sisters and brother would like her or resent her. She would just have to wait and see what happened.

The kids were waking up from there naps, so she went to there rooms to get them up. Cheryl came in about that time and helped her with the kids. They took them down to the kitchen to get some lunch fixed for them.

Lainie told Cheryl that her mom had called earlier and that Leslie and her family were going to come to Colorado to see them. She told her that Leslie said when she made the arrangements, she would let her know.

Cheryl told her she would be there to help her out with everything, not to worry so much. What if my brother and sisters don't like me, Lainie ask Cheryl. Don't worry so much girl, they will love you. What is not to love and with these beautiful children of yours, they will fall in love with them and you too.

Lainie said she sure hopes Cheryl is right. Cheryl told her now the triplets will have and uncle and two aunts and a grandma and another grandpa. She told her that she now has an extended family, and is anxious to meet all of them.

The rest of the week seemed to drag on. Lainie, Jacob and Cheryl took the kids to the water park over the weekend. They all had so much fun. Lainie wanted to make sure the kids all knew how to swim, and she and Cheryl had been teaching them in the pool at home. The kids loved the water, just like Lainie had when she was younger. Between the three adults, it was all they could do to keep up with the kids, and to keep re-applying sunscreen to keep them from getting a sunburn.. The kids were all three, getting brown as little berries. They loved the outdoors, and wanted to go outside all the time.

After getting home that evening, the kids were bathed, fed and put to bed. And were all asleep before there heads hit the pillows. While Laine and Jacob were sitting relaxing with Cheryl, the phone rang, and it was Leslie telling her they would be there on Tuesday. She told Jason was getting off work and coming with them too.

Lainie told her she would have someone pick them up at the airport, but Leslie told her they would rent a car and come to her house. She said I have the address and I am sure we can find it without any problems. She told Lainie there flight came in at 10:45, so we will see you sometime after that. Leslie told Lainie she was nervous about all this and Lainie said she was too. It has been sixteen year since we have seen each other.

— Chapter 19 —

On Tuesday morning, Leslie and her family were all packed and headed to the airport. When the family got there, they had a little bit of a wait until they could board the plane, so they sat and talked. Leslie said she hoped the triplets liked the gifts she had gotten for them.

She had also packed Lainie's old watch. The one she had on when she was taken. Leslie thought she might like to have it back. She had also bought Lainie a new watch, one with diamonds around the face. She just hoped everything would go fine.

She was thinking so hard, that she didn't hear them say they could board the plane now. Jason told her, and she got up and started towards the gate. When she was on board, she got settled in and made sure the kids were all belted in too. Then she just stared out the window and watched the miles fly by. She was so nervous, and lots of things were going through her mind.

She wondered if Lainie would remember her after all these years, and she wondered if she would recognize Lainie . She knew she was all grown up and would look different, but she was still worried somewhat.

The flight seemed like it was over with as soon as it had started. After landing at the Denver airport, and getting there luggage and there rental car, they started out to see

Lainie. Jason told her to just relax, but it was hard for her to do. Jason really did understand what she was going through, and tried to help as much as he could, and so did the kids.

He was glad things had turned out the way they had, and that Lainie was alive and well. He also wondered what would happen when the insurance company found out that Ian had just died a month ago, and not in the car crash as they all had thought. He would cross that bridge when he got to it, and he and Leslie would do it together.

Jason knew that Leslie had gotten a settlement when they thought Ian had dies, but he didn't know how much she had gotten, and had never ask. Of course, it had helped that Ian had never let anyone know that he was still alive, and that is why he continued living up at the cabin all those years. He lived like a hermit, only going into town when he just had too, and not making friends with many people.

Was it up to he and Leslie to tell the insurance company that he was not the man who burned up in the crash, or should they just leave things alone.. That is something he and Leslie would have to discuss when the time was right but now was not that time. They would have to consult a lawyer and find out what there options were on the matter. Ian was at this time deceased, but not like they had thought he had been twenty years ago. He would wait until after they got back form Denver and back in Tennessee before he talked to Leslie about it.

They all got into the rental car and headed in the direction that Lainie's house was in. As they were driving, they were amazed at how different Colorado was from Tennessee. They all liked it from what they could see of it. Of course, there lives were in Tennessee, and they all had jobs and the schooling back there too.

Leslie thought about Lainie then and the kids, and she would like to be somewhere near them , so she could see them more often. That is if things went right for all them while they were here. She could only hope for the best, and go from there.

As they neared the street where the directions told them to go, her butterflies in her stomach were getting worse. She told herself to just calm down, that things would be just fine.

Jason signaled to turn down the street Lainie lived on, and at once realized that the homes here were like mansion. They found the right address and turned in the long winding lane. She thought it was so beautifully landscaped, and then she saw the house, and was in awe of the way it looked. Oh my goodness she said to her family. Jacob must be a very wealthy man to own a home like this. Jason told her to just relax, it was fine.

When they pulled into the drive way, a young woman came out of the house. Leslie looked at her, and immediately knew it was Lainie. They got out of the car and Leslie walked up to Lainie, and said, it really is you, isn't it. Yes, mom it really is me. And you look just like I remembered you. They both hugged and both were crying. Lainie broke free, and said I want to meet my sisters and brother and my step dad too.

Laine told them to get there luggage and come on it, that there rooms were all ready for them, thanks to Cheryl's help. She said, I don't know what I would do without Cheryl here to help me. The kids can be a handful at times, but with her help, we manage to keep them under control. They seem to be into everything all the time, and what one doesn't think about the other ones do.

— Chapter 20 —

After Leslie and her family were settled in, and freshened up, they went down to the kitchen, where Lainie and Cheryl were fixing some lunch for all of them. That was the first time Leslie got to see the grandkids, and as Lainie brought them over to Leslie and Jason, she told the kids that this is your grandma and grandpa, and your aunts and uncle.

Leslie gave the kids each the gifts she had brought for them and then she told Lainie she had something she wanted her to have, and she gave her her watch she had when she was taken. She told Lainie she had kept it all these years, and now she wanted her to have it back. She then gave the new watch to her too.

The kids all three loved there gifts, and were ready to get down and play with them. The kids were all laughing and talking at once. Leslie had to laugh at them, and tried to tell them to talk one at a time, so she could understand what they were saying.

Ellie climbed up on Leslie's lap and told her that Jason is my grandpa now. Ethan spoke up and said grandpa Ian went to Heaven, and he can't play with us anymore. He ask Jason, will you play with us like grandpa Ian use to do? He then ask Laura, Lane and Jay if they would play with them too. He told them they could go swimming if they wanted to, that is if mommy and Cheryl is out there with us.

Jason felt a knot in his throat, and told Ethan that he and his aunt and uncle would love to play with them, but that no one could ever replace grandpa Ian. Jason picked up Ethan and was rewarded with a big hug from the little boy. Emily and not were not going be left out so they said hug for us too.

Leslie couldn't get over how much the three kids looked like Lainie when she was there age.

Jacob came home later that day to find the three kids in the yard with Lainie, Cheryl, Leslie, Jason, Jay, Laura and Lane. Jay was down the ground playing with the kids while the girls watched and the adults talked.

Leslie told Lainie about the day she didn't return home when she was suppose to, and how she felt it was her fault for letting her go to the park by herself. I got to the park and looked everywhere for you. I called your friends mom and she told me her girls were home and that you were still at the park when her girls left.

She told me Joanie and Jill had been home since 2:00, and they told her Lainie said she was going to play and then go home at 3:00.

I called the police and they sent an officer over to try to help find you, but you were not there. I walked over all the park and to the swings and the pond. When I was at the swing, I found your watch laying in the grass by the swings.

I told the police what I had found, and they then called the canine unit into try to find a scent for you, so they could track you. When Lainie saw her old watch, she gasped, and said she always wondered where it had gone to. She said I remember checking the time just before someone grabbed me. He put his hand over my mouth so I wouldn't scream, and he told me he wasn't going to hurt me.

He took me to his van that was in the parking area. Then he opened the door and put me in the seat, and buckled my seatbelt, and told me we were going to take ride. That my mom wanted him to take me and keep me with him.

I told him I just wanted to go hom, and he told me, we are going home, and called me sweetheart.

With that he got into the van and we drove off. I must have fallen asleep, and when I woke up, he ask me if I was hungry. We stopped at a McDonalds and got some hamburgers and drinks, the headed on down the road.

I ask him where we were going, but he wouldn't tell me. I pushed my hair back out of my eyes, and that was when I noticed I had lost one of my hair barrettes too. I looked around in the seat for it, but it wasn't there.

We drove for two days, and only stopped to get gas and something to eat, and to use the restroom. Ian would stop at a rest area and lay his head down and sleep for a couple of hours, then back to driving he went

I was asleep when we finally got to the cabin, so I didn't see where we were going to. Ian carried me in and laid me down on the couch. I guess I sleep until the next morning, cause the sun was coming through the window when I woke up.

I was scared when I woke up, cause I didn't know where I was at. Ian was up fixing breakfast for us. I ask him where I was , and he told me we were at his dad's cabin in the woods. He said his dad and mom use to come up here all the time, and now it was his since they both were dead. I have been living here now for about four years. It is nice and quiet and peaceful here.

Ian was really very nice to me al he gave me everything I needed and even home schooled me. He would take me to town and buy me clothes. He told me, I was growing like a weed.

When he gave me this locket, he told me he would tell me who they were. And he did when I was twenty one. Leslie ask if she could see the locket, so Lainie gave it to her to see. Leslie looked at the pictures inside and said that is Ian's dad and mom in that picture. They loved you when you were first born, but then about a year later, your grandma died and with in a few months your grandpa was gone too. It was as if he couldn't live without her.

My mom and dad, your grandparents were so devastated when you were taken, and they are so glad that you are okay and they want to see you soon too. I had to call them to tell them that you were alive and that Ian, who we all thought was dead, had taken you to his dad's cabin in Colorado.

Leslie said she would call and let them know it really is you, and that they are great grandparents. Lanine ask if her grandparents still lived on Ohio. Leslie told her they had moved to Tennessee to be closer to her and Jason and the family. We love having them near by.

— Chapter 21 —

The kids were getting tired, but as soon as they saw there daddy, they all seemed to get an extra boost of energy. Daddy, daddy, daddy, all three of them yelled and ran to meet him. He scooped all three of them up and gave them hugs and kisses. He ask them if they were having fun, and they all said "yes", we are paying with grandpa Jason, and uncle Jay, and aunts, Laura and Lane.

Jacob walked over to Jason who had gotten off the ground where the kids were playing. He help out his hand to Jason, and said he was sorry he wasn't there when they first got there, but I know Lainie and Cheryl had taken good care of you. I had that meeting, that I had to be at, but I am here now, and plan on being here with all of you while you are here.

He told Jason he was so happy to finally meet Lainie's mom and her family. Jason said that he and Leslie we so glad to find out that Lainie was alive and well, and not what they had thought all those years, and of course to see she has a great husband and three great kids makes it all worth while.

He told Jacob about all the years Leslie thought Lainie was dead and that she would never see her again. She was so beside herself when she got the news, she just couldn't believe it. She was a little skeptical about all this, and kept asking me if I thought this was for real or just some ones idea of a cruel joke.

After she talked to Lainie over the phone, she was certain that it was Lainie she was talking to, because only the two of them would know what had happened that day.

The police dept had not told anyone about finding the watch or the hair barrette, and that was the one thing Lainie told her about when they talked.

It is really ashamed though that Ian died, but I a glad he told Lainie who he was and how to get in touch with her mom, through the police department. I now he must have loved her very much to do what he did for her. From what Lainie has told us about him, he was a wonderful man. She was lucky to have had him in her life.

Jacob and Jason walked over to where Lainie, Leslie, and Cheryl were sitting talking.

Cheryl was talking about Ian when they walked up. She told them that Ian loved Lainie so much and he thought the sun rose and sat in her, and in there grandchildren. She said he was the best person she had ever met. She said the only regret was that he died so young, and that they didn't have much time together.

She said Ian had told her all about Leslie and then about the car crash that he was supposedly to have died in, and that for two years he had had amnesia, and couldn't remember who he was. One morning, he woke up at the and it was at that time he started remembering things, and who he was.

He drove to the library and got on the computers and looked up any information he could find and he found the story of the crash and that the car had burned the body so badly they had no way to identify who was in it, and they just supposed it was his body.

He remembered that day picking up a male hitchhiker, and that neither of them had on there seatbelts. He remembered taking the curve to fast, and losing control of the car, and just as the car was going over the cliff, he jumped out. Someone had picked him up and had taken him to the hospital, but the car was so far down the cliff, no one could see it from where they were at.

He was in the hospital for a week, and still had no idea who he was or where he lived or anything like that.

The story said the car was spotted by a plane flying over the area, and called it into the police. The story said the car was registered to Ian, and since they thoughthe was in the car, that it was his body they recovered.

Cheryl said a story in a later edition said that the insurance company had paid a claim for his death to Leslie, and he knew it was for $100,000 . He learned later that Leslie had bought the house there in Allenville, Ohio with the money.

Ian didn't want to mess things up for Leslie or Lainie, so he said he just stayed up at the cabin, so no one would know he was still alive. He thought about them all the time, and he went to Allenville to see if he could find them, but he had grown his hair long and had a beard, so no one noticed him, and besides it was a different town than they had lived in together.

About four years had passed and he went back to Allenville, and he saw Lainie and he would watch her from a distance, and he wanted her to be with him, so when he saw her alone in the park that day, he decided to take her with him. He had it all planned out to take her back to the cabin where no one would be looking for them there.

Cheryl said Ian wanted Lainie to know the whole story about what he had done, and why. He said he was sorry that Leslie has to go through what she went through, but he had no choice. He didn't want to just come back from the dead and since Leslie had received all the insurance money and he knew she had no way to pay it back . He thought he was protecting her too as far as that matter went.

He said he couldn't tell her until he was on his death bed, but he did tell her everything before he died.

— Chapter 22 —

Lainie sat very still and she had tears falling down her check. She said she had loved Ian, and wasn't sorry that he had done what he had. Her only regret was that her mom didn't know she was alive and doing well.

Lainie told them all about fishing, and swimming in the lakes and streams around the cabin. She said they would have to go up there one day so she could show them where she lived with Ian. She also told them the blue van was till parked in the trees behind the cabin too.

She told them Ian taught her to drive in the Jeep he had bought. I always felt love when I was with him, and I think I always knew he was my dad. I know I was only four when he was supposed to have died, but I still remembered things about him.

— Chapter 23 —

Leslie and Jason ask if Jacob, Lainie and Cheryl and three kids would like to come for a visit to Tennessee, That way they could see where they lived and see the beautiful hills there too.

Lainie said they would do just that, and then Jacob told them he might just look around and buy a house there so Lainie and all of them could come see them more often. Lainie said she wanted to get to know more about her sisters and her brother now too.

They had all had so much fun there in Denver with Jacob and Lainie, and of course Cheryl was great to them too, and they considered her family too.

Leslie told her that Jay is nineteen, and Laura is sixteen and Lane is six, and they love the three little kids. Lainie told Jacob that a house there in Tennessee would be great. She wanted her kids to know there aunts and uncle.

They all talked that afternoon while the kids took there naps. Leslie told them that the police had found her hair barrette in the parking lot where it had fallen out of her hair. She told them the police brought dogs in, but couldn't find anything with her scent on it to follow. She said the man who was fishing in the pond told them he had seen a blue van and a man with a ball cap on and it was red and had the letter "R" on the front of it.

Lainie said , yes, I remember that cap. Dad wore it most of the time when we went fishing. I don't know what happened to it though. Cheryl laughed, and said, honey it is in the house in one of those boxes I packed up with your dads stuff in it. I hadn't decided what to do with his things, and if you want them, you can have them. I guess he left most of his clothes at the cabin. I would like to go up there some day.

Lainie said, well why don't we all just load and drive up there in the morning. Cheryl, we can pack a picnic to eat and we can explore. Everyone will absolutely love it there.

It was decided they would leave around seven the next morning, so they could get there since it was a two hour drive. Next morning, they all loaded into the conversion van where there was room for all of the family to ride together.

The drive up Leslie and Jason said it was as beautiful there as it is in Tennessee, and Lainie told them to wait until they get to the cabin and see how pretty it is there.

The closer they got to the cabin, the more Lainie thought she was coming home. She had always loved the seclusion and the sheer beauty of the area.

When they pulled into the long lane, the trees were so green and smelled so good. Leslie said this is so nice up here. The cabin came into view and they van stopped, and the kids were all wanting outside to play.

Ethan was running towards the cabin and Emily and Ellie were right on his tail. Although they had never been here before, Ethan said, this is where grandpa Ian lived, I see his fishing poles, he told me about them.

I want to go fishing, can we mom? Lainie laughed, and ask Ethan how he knew this was grandpa Ian's? Because mommy, he told me he and you use to go fishing and I see the fishing poles, and I know the little one is yours. Can I take it and go fishing to? Please mommy?

Lainie told him to wait for a few minutes and they would take them down to the stream to fish. Ethan said he wanted to catch a fish so they could eat it for lunch, Of course Emily and Ellie were not going be left out, and they said they wanted to catch a fish too.

They finally calmed the kids down and went inside the cabin. Lainie showed them where her bed was up in the loft, also the bedroom where Ian slept. The cabin smelt a little musty since no one had been there for about two years now.

Lainie opened the windows and the breeze started blowing through and got the musty smell out quickly.

They all went back outside and Lainie showed Leslie the blue van that was used when Ian picked her up that day.

They took the poles off the porch and headed for the stream. The kids were having so much fun. They found wil flowers and picked one each for Lainie, Leslie and Cheryl. When they reached the stream, the kids let out a squeal, and said "me go fishing"

After the poles were ready, and the lines thrown into the water, the adults sat down with the kids. The first pole bent, and it had a fish on it. Ethan was so excited, he grabbed the pole and pulled. Jacob, who was beside Ethan told him what to do, and with his help, Ethan reeled the fish in. It was a good sized fish and Jacob got it up with the net they had. Ethan yelled, look mom I caught a fish, mom , take him off so I can catch another one.

No sooner than Ethan's fish was off his line Emily yelled that she had a fish too. That was when Lainie got to her and then Ellie said she had one too. Lainie took both girls fish off there hooks and when they had there poles back into the water, she sat down and laughed. The kids caught about three more fish each, and then they were told that would be enough for lunch, so they had to get them back to the cabin and clean them.

The kids were disappointed they couldn't fish longer, but they all three minded there mom and dad.

Lainie told then she wanted to show them where she use to swim, so they walked down to the lake. It was so clear and the water was so blue, that you could see the bottom for a long ways out.

Leslie and Cheryl were in awe when they saw the lake. They just couldn't get over the fact that the water was so clear, and they both walked out into the lake up to there knees. The water was cool and so clean. It is no wonder you loved it so much here Lainie, I would have too.

Maybe one day, we can all come back for a weekend and bring a couple of campers and all of us can have a nice place to sleep and enough room to enjoy all this beauty. It is so unspoiled and spectacular here. Just let us know when you all want to come..

After coming back from the lake, they stopped and got the fish out of the stream still attached to the stringer. The water was so nice and cool that the fish were not hurt at all.. When they got to the cabin, Lainie went ahead and cleaned and filleted the fish and got them ready to cook over the fire.

The kids were playing in the yard in front of the cabin while Leslie and Cheryl watched them. Lainie got the fire ready and started frying the fish. When all of it was done, she took it back outside to where the picnic table had been set up with the rest of the food they had brought.

They all sat down to eat, and everyone loved the fish, even the kids. Ethan said I want to catch more fish. We did good, didn't we mommy? She told him they could catch more fish when they came back again. The kids all said they liked it here at grandap Ian 's cabin.

After the meal was over and things were cleaned back up, Jacob said they needed to start back home.

Leslie said she remembered Ian telling her right after they were married, about the cabin his dad built, but I didn't remember where he said it was. He had said one summer, they were going to come up here for a couple of weeks, but that was the month before he was supposed to have died in the car crash.

I wish he had gotten in touch with me when his memory came back, and we could have worked things out with the insurance company. I guess he remembered all the fights he and I had before the crash happened and maybe he just didn't want to come back for that reason. Things just might have been different, but I guess, we have a reason why we do the things we do. I am happy now, since I have my baby girl back..

The kids were all back into there booster seats and the van was on the way back home. All three kids had worn themselves out and all three were sound asleep about five minutes after they were buckled in.

They woke up about half an hour from home, and Emily said she wanted ice cream, and Ellie and Ethan said "me too' Jacob stopped and everyone got ice cream. They all sat at one of the tables that was in the shade of an oak tree eating there ice cream. When the kids were done, and wiped off, and back into there seats , they were on there way home.

— Chapter 24 —

When they got home. Leslie told Lainie she wanted to talk to her, so Laine said that was fine. They sat on the patio drinking iced tea. Leslie started with how sorry she was that she could never find Lainie. She said not a day went by that she didn't think about her and wonder. She told her how she had called the Allenville police department about every two weeks, then every month since she had disappeared.

I felt so helpless and I blamed myself for letting you go to that park alone. I just though since Allenville was such a small town and nothing bad ever happened there. I thought you would be safe. I am so sorry Lainie.

Please don't cry mom. We are together now, and I was never in any way harmed while I was with dad.

I know it must have been hard on you, not knowing where I was, or even if I was alive or dead. Don't blame yourself, cause you had nothing to do with this. Dad said you ask him to take me because you needed to get some things worked out and then you would call me. That is what I believed all those years.

As the years went by, I guess I forgot , or just figured you still had problems to figure out. I was happy, and was safe. I was having fun at the cabin and it was just like being on vacation.

It is me who should be sorry. I didn't insist on calling you, but dad told me you had remarried and had a new family now. I guess I thought you didn't want me anymore.

Oh honey, never think that. I will always love you, nothing will ever stop that. I am glad that Ian told you everything before he died. He was always a good person.

I am sorry that he is gone, but I thought I had lost him when you were four years old. It was rough for a while, and then the I finally got the insurance check, and that is what I used to buy the house we were living in there in Allenville.

For two years, I stayed there searching for you. Then I met Jason at work one day, HE was a sales representative from Tennessee. We dated for a year, and he ask me to marry him.

I sold the house in Allenville, and moved to Tennessee with Jason, but I before I moved, I went to the police and gave them my new address and phone number in case they found out anything about you.

A year after we were married, we had Jay, then three years after that we had Laura. I thought I was done having babies, and then ten years later, We had Lane. I have already told you that we named her after you, She had the same blonde hair and same color eyes you had.

— Chapter 25 —

The day the police called me to tell me about your call to them and them coming out to see and talk to you. That day was the day I had prayed for all my life. I just couldn't believe my ears. I ask them if they were sure, and they said they had done some DNA testing to make sure that you were who you said you were.

They had taken your hair brush and toothbrush so they could do some DNA on file just in case they found you or your body.

Yes, Lainie said, I remember them asking me if I would give them a DNA sample. I told them it was fine with me.

They called me back the next day and told me that they were sure that I was the same girl they had been looking for all these years. They told me they had called you and gave you all the information and that you were going to call me some time later.

I am so glad you did call me, and now my life is almost complete. What do you mean Leslie said by almost complete? Well Lainie said, I want to get to know my brother and my sisters better.. I know they are having a hard time with all this, but I think it will all work out in the long run. I know they adore the triplets, so that is half the battle right there.

Leslie said she hope they all could come to Tennessee real soon. Lainie told her that they would all come with the next two months.

Cheryl , Lainie and Leslie were in the kitchen fixing dinner. Jacob and Jason had the three little ones outside playing with Jay, Laura, and Lane helping watch them.

When dinner was almost ready, Leslie called them all in. She washed the kids up and brought them into the kitchen. The kids had started calling her and Cheryl both Nana. Leslie loved hearing them talk. They each had there own personalities, but in a way they were all the same.

They never fought with each other and they shared everything. The only time they cried was when they fell down outside, other than that they were a well adjusted threesome.

At dinner, Leslie ask Jacob if there had been twins or triplets on his side of the family. He said his grandmother had been a twin, but that her sister had dies when she was two years old. I don't remember of any other twins and no triplets born on my side of the family.

Of course, you know my mom passed away from caner, and my dad died in a car wreck. Leslie cringed at the words he said about the car wreck. It brought back so many memories to her. She had to put those memories aside for now, because she knew they were not real.

Jacob realized what he had said about his dads car wreck, and knew it had brought the memories of when she thought Ian had died the same way. He told her he was so sorry for bringing back up the bad memories for her, but he was just trying to tell her about his family.

My mom has a sister and two brothers, and they all live out in Arizona. My dad was an only child, as I am. After I was big enough to know about things she told me they had wanted more kids, but every time she got pregnant, she miscarried, so after four time, she just gave up hope. The doctor told her it was to hard on her body and he wouldn't advise her to try to have any more kids. So that is why I am an only child. She told me she was on bed rest for the last three months when she was pregnant with me. So you see, she even had problems at that time too.

When my dad died, he left everything to me. He and I had worked side by side for a few years. I started going to the office with him when I was sixteen. My summer vacations were spent there too. Dad wanted me to learn the business inside out, so one day when he retired, I could take over for him.

After mom dies, he was so depressed that I ended up taking care of the business on a daily basis. I would go to school and then straight home and start on the business. On the weekends, I was always in the office finishing things up for the week, and starting things for the next. I never had time to date anyone because of my schedule.

After dad died, I decided I need a small break, but it was business too. We had some companies in Rome who were lagging a bit, so I made plans to go over to see what I could do to help them out some.

It was my lucky trip, because that is where I met Lainie and Ian. The first time I glanced at Lainie, I knew I wanted her for my wife. She was so beautiful and yet so down to earth. She knew the language so well, I thought hat she was a native of Rome.

When I said hello to her in Italian, she said hi back to me in English. I ask her where she was from, and she told me she and Ian lived in Colorado. I told her I was from Colorado myself.

We talked for hours and I invited her and Ian to dinner that night. She told me she and Ian lived in this cabin that was so isolated, and in the woods. She said she loved it there.

I ask her when they were going back home, and she told me they were leaving on Saturday. I told her that is when I was heading back home too. When she told me her flight, I told her I was on the same flight. She said there seats were in coach, and I ask if they would care if I paid for an upgrade to first class, then we could all set together on the flight home.

Ian wasn't very keen on the idea, but Lainie said that she would like to do that, so Ian agreed to do just that. He always like to pay his own way, but this time he gave in because he knew Lainie wanted it.

When he called the airport, they told Jacob they had plenty of first class seats available, and they were all in the section where his seats were, so he thought that was great. Come Saturday, they all boarded and Lainie sat next t him and Ian sat on the other side of her.

The flight was very smooth and when they talked out, they all took a nap. The flight was twelve hours long, so it was nice to be able to lean back and sleep for a while. After they landed, Jacob ask Ian and Lainie if they wanted to come by his house and spend the night, because he knew they had a two hour trip yet to get home.

They came to the house, and they met Cheryl. I could tell she was taken in by Ian. Her eyes lit up when she saw him. She showed them to there rooms and came back to finish making dinner. Jacob had called ahead and told her he was bringing company home, for dinner and they were going to spend the night with them.

Jacob came back down after freshening up and Cheryl said, Lainie is such a beautiful girl, you need to marry that one. I told her that was exactly what he had in mind.

After dinner was over, Lainie said she was going to help Cheryl clean things back up. She knew Cheryl was watching Ian, and that he had been watching her too.

That night Lainie was walking to her bedroom, and Jacob came out of a room two doors down from hers. He walked up to her and they talked for a while then he leaned down and kissed her.

Her legs got real shaky and she had to put her arms around him to keep from falling. She made it to her bed and sat down. When they got ready to leave, Jacob kissed her again, and told her , he would see her real soon.

Anyway, Jacob went to the cabin where Lainie and Ian we living, and ask her to marry him. He ask her and Ian to move back with him to the house, and they both agreed.

Jacob told Ian he wanted to date Lainie, and he wanted to marry her too.

So Ian and Lainie packed up there things and moved in with me, then in April, Lainie and I were married, and we went to Hawaii on our honeymoon for three weeks, but had to cut things short because Lainie got sick, so we came home. She went to the doctor and found out she was pregnant. It wasn't until a few months later, we found out she was carrying triplets. We were both so happy and I an was very excited about the news.

Ian and Cheryl go very close and by the time the babies were born, they were married too. So as you can see, Leslie and Jason, it has been a whirlwind around. We are so glad to have you and your family here with us too.

— Chapter 26 —

So Jason, what type of work are you into? He told them what he does back in Tennessee, and that Jay is also working with him too. He is doing just a wonderful job.

Leslie told them she works part time at the school Lane goes to. That way, I am home when Lane is there. I guess I am still a little paranoid thinking about someone taking her. Lainie told her not to worry about that, it was no stranger who took me, and I am safe so don't worry so much.

Lainie was sad when it was time for Leslie and her family to leave, but she promised

Then they would come out and visit the next month. In the meantime, we can keep in touch by phone. Now that I have found you again, I don't want to lose you again Leslie said to her.

— Chapter 27 —

The weatherman was calling for storms overnight, and into the next day. Lainie knew her mom and family were leaving to go home tomorrow. She hoped the weather would clear up before they had to leave. She knew Leslie hated flying in the storms.

That was not to be because it stormed all night long, and as morning came, it was still at it. The rain was coming down so hard, they thought it might start flooding. Leslie and her family hated to leave but they had to get back home with there kids. They all kissed and hugged everybody, and then headed to the airport. It was raining so hard, the flight got delayed for an hour.

Leslie called back home and her mom answered the phone, because her mom and dad had stayed there to watch the house while the family was gone. She told her mom that Lainie was great, and that she had plenty of pictures to show her when she got home. After the hour delay, the storm was still raging outside, so they had another delay. Jason told Leslie not to worry, that the rain would quit soon, but not to be surprised if it didn't hear east after leaving Colorado.

Finally, the storm broke enough for them to board the pane and get airborne headed home. They still rain into some rain on the flight home, but it wasn't too bad at all.

They just had some spots were it was bumpy and they had to keep there seatbelts fastened most of the flight.

Jason was right about the rain moving east, because by the time they landed in Tennessee, it was raining there too. It was not raining as hard as it had in Colorado, but it was a light rain. The got there luggage and were on there way home very shortly after getting off the plane. They were just two hours later than there original flight had be scheduled.

When they pulled up in front of the house, her mom came out to help them with the luggage, and by the time all of them got back into the house, it cut loose and just started to pour the rain..

Leslie told her mom about everything that she could about Lainie. She showed them the pictures she had taken. Her mom was so happy to finally see her great grandchildren, and thought they were so cute.

I sure would love to see them her mom said. Leslie told her that Lainie and Jacob and Cheryl were bringing the triplets there sometime next month. She told her mom that Lainie said they were going to try to buy a house near them, so they could watch the babies grow up too. She said she wants to know her step sisters and step brother better and she wants them to know her kids too. She wanted her kids to know there grandparents and great grand parents, aunts and uncle.

— Chapter 28 —

Jacob flew to Tennessee the week after Leslie, Jason and there family went home , and he looked at several houses, but none were what he wanted, but he did find some land he really like, then found a contractor and had him start to build a home for his family. Jacob told him what he wanted and the contractor started on it the same day. The house was to be done within the month. The contractor kep in touch with Jacob on the progress of the house. The land had ten acres on it, big enough to have a pool and a guest house like they have at the one in Colorado.

Next Jacob went to an interior designer and had them furnish the whole house just like he knew Lainie would want it to be furnished. When the house was done and the furnishing all in place, then is when he told Lainie what he had done, and that they had a house now to go to when they went to Tennessee to stay for a while.

When it was all done he told Lainie that there was even enough room for Cheryl, because she was part of the family to and she had to go with them when they went to visits.

Jacob was so pleased with the way everything was proceeding and there were no problems encountered in the process. When the contractor called to let him know that everything was ready to go and he could bring his family at anytime, that everything was all set, and they even had all the kitchen stocked with everything he said he wanted in it.

He and Lainie and Cheryl started making plans to go to there new home for a visit. She was anxious to see her grandparents too. She called Leslie and told her they were coming out and that Jacob had had a house built just for them and then she told Leslie where it was located. Leslie said, that is just about a mile from us here then. She told her they would be out in a few days.

Cheryl helped packed the kids clothing for a two month stay in Tennessee, They each had to put a favorite top and shorts in too. Emily and Ellie each had to pack a stuffed rabbit that they like to sleep with, while Ethan had a brown teddy bear he had to take. They were growing so fast and probably by the end of the two months, they would have to have new clothes.

Lainie had taught all three of them how to swim. She called them her water babies. They loved being in the pool, and were getting so brown. Cheryl helped Lainie with them while they were in the pool.

Cheryl remembered the times when she and Ian would skinny dip in the pool when no one else was around. She only wished she could have had more time with him. She knew Lainie missed him a lot too, but she had the kids to keep her busy. Oh, the memories are all I have now of him, but they are good ones.

— Chapter 30 —

The family, along with Cheryl flew to Tennessee on Jacobs private plane. They had a car waiting at the airport to transport them to there new home.

The driveway was a long and winding one to the house. When Lainie first saw the house, she couldn't believe it. It was almost identical to the house in Colorado, even down to the pool and the guest house..

Oh, Jacob, she said, with tears rolling down her cheeks, it is beautiful. Jacob just smiles and hugged her and told her only wanted the best for her. When they went inside, she loved the way it was decorated. She went into the kitchen, which was a state of the art kitchen. Everything a cook could want. She opened the cabinet doors to find they were fully stocked with everything she would want or need to fix there meals.

Next she walked upstairs to fine the triplets rooms were so cozy. They girls rooms had small canopy beds in them with white and pink lace curtains. Ethan's room had a race car bed in it, and black and white checked curtains. All three kids squealed with delight at there rooms, and there beds.

When everyone was settled in and lunch was over with, Lainie put in a call to Leslie to let her know they had arrived just fine, It was a surprise to Leslie, because Lainie hadn't told her about the house yet.   She told Leslie they had to come over to see the house and for dinner the next evening.

Leslie agreed and Lainie gave her the address, and the new phone number for the house.

All the next day, Lainie and Cheryl were preparing the food they were going to serve that evening. Cheryl baked a chocolate cake for dessert. She put chocolate curls on top of the frosting. It looked to pretty to but, but Lainie knew it would be delicious.

Late afternoon, Lainie and Cheryl bathed the triplets and put clean clothes on them, and they ere all ready to see grandma and grandpa and there aunts and uncle.

When Leslie and her family got to the house, Lane was the first to the door. She was so excited to see the triplets again. She gave Lainie a hug, as did Leslie and Jason. Next she gave Laura and Jay a hug too and told them all to come inside that the triplets were wanting to see them all.

The triplets were running into the room, and yelling hi to everyone.. Ellie wanted to be the attention getter, but Ethan was not going to let her out do him, He ran to Leslie, and she bent down to pick him up. He said hi to Lane, Laura and Jay. Ethan asked Jay if her wanted to go swimming with him and Jay grinned and sure buddy, let's go outside and see your pool, then we can ask your mom if it is ok with her.

Of course, when the word swim was mentioned, all three kids said , please mommy, can we go swimming. Lainie said it would ok if they were good, and all three said they would be really good.

Emily's long hair had come out of its barrette, so Laura reached down, and told her she would fix it for her. After the barrette was back in her hair, she gave Laura a hug, and said, thank you Aunt Laura.

Ellie grabbed Lane by the hand, and said come see me doll house in my room, and Emily said, it is mine too. So with Ellie on side and Emily on the other, they headed up the stairs. The girls stayed in there room until Leslie called them down to dinner.

Ellie and Emily loved playing with Lane, and she loved being with them too. At dinner, the kids chattered non stop. They thought it was so much fun to have everyone there with them again.

They enjoyed the food, and when Cheryl brought out the chocolate cake, the kids yelled, me, me, me, I want some. Cheryl gave them a small piece and then cut some for the adults.

When the kids were done, they had cake all over there faces, and hands too. After getting them cleaned back up, Ethan ask Jay if he wanted to go back out to swim again. Lainie told Jay to watch him really close.

When they got to the pool, Ethan wanted to show Jay how well he could swim, so he took off across the pool. Ethan swam very well, and Jay was impressed at how much better he had gotten since they were out to Colorado. They swam for a while then got out. After drying off, and getting changed back into there clothes, they went in the house to be with the rest of the family.

— Chapter 31 —

Leslie and Lainie thought things were going really well, and that her brother and sisters got along so well with the triplets. Lainie thought her mom and Jason had done a great job raising the three kids they had together, and she was happy for them.

Everyone but Lainie and Leslie had gone outside, so they started talking again She ask Leslie if she had tried to find her, and if she ever wondered if she was alive or dead. Did you ever think it might have been dad who tool me. Did you wonder how I would look and what kind of a person I turned out to be. I guess with three kids of my own now, it makes me more curious as to why the police never found anything that would lead them to me.

Leslie sat with tears dropping of her cheeks. She said, Lainie, I tried myself to find you for two years straight. You were never off my mind even for a minute. There no clues as to where you were or who had taken you.

The older man, Larry, who had been fishing in the pond that day, couldn't tell us anything more than a man in a blue van had taken you, but he thought it was your dad picking you up. He said the man had on a red baseball cap with a big "R" on the front. That was all he could remember. He said he never even looked at the license plate on the van.

I never once suspected your dad of taking you, because I thought he had died in the car wreck four years before that.

I had no reason to go to the cabin there in Colorado, because without you, my whole world was lost. I don't even think I thought about that cabin, because we had never been there.

When I met Jason, he helped me cope with everything, and he even helped me look for you. Between the both of us, we drove around every town within a thirty mile radius around Allenville hunting for you.

I cried so much and was so depressed, the doctor wanted to put me on medication, but I refused. All I wanted was to have you back safe and sound where you belonged.

After a year with Jason, he asked me to marry him, and since he had been so good to me and I loved him very much, I said yes.

A year later Jay was born, then two years after that I had Laura. No one could ever replace you though Lainie. Then ten years later, we were surprised to find out I was pregnant with Lane. Jason and I talked after we found out she was a girl, and we decides to name her Lane Marie, after her sister. I was hoping that one day she would be able to meet you, and know that she was named after you.

I told all three of the kids about you being taken, and that one day I hoped you would get in touch with me, That was the happiest day of my life when the detective called to tell me you were alive, and living in Colorado.

Lainie couldn't be more happy than she is now. There is one thing she missed a lot, and that was Ian. He was so good to me, mom, and I had everything I ever wanted. He kept me fed, and he home schooled me. I think he was the smarted man I have ever known. He took me to get clothes, and always let me get what I wanted no matter the cost. He told me he wanted me to be happy. I told him I didn't need a lot of expensive things to make me happy.

He kept me busy with the schooling, and I even helped him saw down some trees, and chopped some wood. I could fish as well as he could, and most of the time, I caught more fish than he did.

He taught me how to swim, and float in the lake. You saw how beautiful it was and how clear the water was. I guess I took to the water like a fish myself.

At night, we would sit out on the porch at the cabin, and heat the animals in the woods playing, and the deer were so use to us , they would come up to eat out of our hands. It was so calm and peaceful out there.

I loved to read, so Ian would take me to the library once a week. I would get lots of books, and in the summer, I would read at least three books a week.

Some of the books were study ones. That is how I learned to speak several different languages. Ian and I would both read them and learn. We would talk to each other in Italian and Spanish. I even got him to speaking German to. It was lots of fun for both of us.

— Chapter 32 —

Leslie said, it sounds like you had a good life with your dad. I feel like I was deprived of seeing you grow up and become a beautiful woman you are today though.

When we all thought Ian had died in the wreck, my whole world stopped. Here I was with a four year old, and only worked part time at the local grocery store. I had no skills and no college degree. About two weeks after the crash, and insurance company got in touch with me to tell me Ian had a life insurance policy worth $500,000, and that it would be given to me since I was the sole beneficiary of the policy.

So one week later, I got the check from the insurance company, and I bought the house we lived in there in Allenville. I put money in the bank and had a fund set up for your college education. We didn't live extravagant, and no one knew we had the money.

When you were taken, I waited for a ransom call to come in, the police even had my phone tapped just in case, but the call never came.. The days that followed were a blur to me. I was just barely functioning and trying to get through each day.

After a year, and still no word or nothing being found. It seemed like you had just vanished off the face of the earth.

All I could think about was that you had been raped and killed and was in an unmarked grave somewhere.

When I first saw your face that day, everything came back and I just thanked God for keeping you safe. I saw that pretty blonde hair, and those the progressive photo the had done, was exactly what I saw, and I knew you were my Lainie, and that you were alive.

Lainie told Leslie she remembered the day she was taken very well. You were planting flowers in the flower bed, and I wanted to go play in the park with Joanie and Jill. They were my best friends, so you let me go, but told me to be home by three. Joanie and Jill and I played, and we walked over to the pond to look, then went to play on the slides.

They both had watches on, so they saw it was two o'clock, they said they had to go home. I remember telling them goodbye, and then walked over to the swings and was swinging.

I never saw the man coming up to the swings until he grabbed hold of me. I looked down at my wrist, and saw it was two fifteen. That was when his hand slide down my arm and the watch must have fallen off.

He carried me to the van and opened the passenger door and put me in the seat, and put the seatbelt on me. He told me that you had ask him to pick me up , and to take me with him because you had to go out of town and had to leave in a hurry, and didn't know when you would be back.

I though he told me was true, so I just sat in the van, and he got into the drivers seat, and we left the park.

We drove until it got dark and he had two sleeping bags in the back, so he found someplace and we pulled off and stopped. He got us something to eat and we used the bathroom, then got back into the van and drove to a parking lot and got into the sleeping bags and went to sleep. Ian was awake long before I was, and when I woke up, we were moving again.

That evening is when we got to the cabin. Ian fixed us something to eat, then we went to sleep. He told me the loft was where I would be sleeping, so I climbed up there.

He told me that tomorrow he would take me to the store and buy me some clothes since mom didn't have time to pack my clothes for him to bring to me. I thought you didn't want me with you, so I never questioned what I an told me.

— Chapter 33 —

Oh, honey, I am so sorry. I never wanted to be without you. I prayed every night and day the police would find you. I know Ian didn't stop to think what it would do to me.

He had to have known I got the money from his insurance policy, and didn't want to take the chance that I would have to repay the money if they knew he was still alive. For that I thank him. I could never have repaid all the money, since I had used some of it to buy our house.

With him living in the cabin, no one would have know he was alive. I hat him for taking you, but I am glad he treated you so good.. He always loved you so much, and you were very much a daddy's girl. You would always sit on the step in nice weather to wait for him to get home. When the weather was bad, you sat by the window to watch for him.

The day of the crash, you waited on the steps until the police came to inform me of what had happened. I had to make you come in the house. You just kept saying you were waiting for daddy. I told you he wasn't coming home and that he had gone to Heaven. You were only four years old and you wanted to get in the car and go to Heaven so you could see daddy.

It took days for you to understand that daddy was with Jesus up in Heaven in the sky. You cried yourself to sleep for two weeks. You still st at the window and waited though every day for a week.

I just wish things had been different back then. I wish I had had them do an autopsy on the body, but I thought your dad was the only one in the car. Someone, somewhere lost a son and they don't even know what happened to him. I had the remains cremated since the body was burned beyond recognition. If only I had know..

Don't beat yourself up mom, no one ever knew, and I didn't really know for sure, but I had my suspicions, but didn't know for sure until the day he told me before he died.

He told me everything mom, and you were right about him not wanting the insurance company to know he was still alive. He knew you had received the money. So he stayed away for that reason.

He wanted me to tell you he loved you, and hated to see you hurt. He didn't like not being able to see me, so he planned to take me and keep me where no one would even think about looking me for.

He wanted me to tell you he was sorry. He wished he could have taken you with us too, but he knew it would be impossible without the FBI getting involved. He kept tabs on you all those years. He wanted to be able to tell me everything I needed to know when the time came, so I could find you.

— Chapter 34 —

The family came back in about that time and Leslie said they needed to get back home. Laura told Lainie if she needed a sitter when they were here in Tennessee, just to call her. She said she would be delighted to watch the triplets anytime. They are such little darling. Lane said she would help too. Ethan told Jay he wanted him t come back and swim with him again.

After Leslie and Jason and the family left, Lainie and Cheryl took the kids up for another bath, when Emily ran to Jacob and gave him a big kiss and hug and told him goodnight. After baths were over with, they were put to bed. They all had had such a big day, and were tired. Emily and Ellie both said they liked Aunt Laura and Aunt Lane and wanted them to come over every day to play with them. Lainie told them not to worry, that they would see there aunts really often.

There last day in Tennessee, the whole family was together. They took the kids to the zoo and had a picnic in the park at the zoo.

Goodbyes were said and Lainie and Jacob and Cheryl along with the triplets all headed to the airport. They flew back home on Jacob's private jet. The kids were so tired they all fell asleep on the flight home.

Jacob ask Lainie if she had fun and how she liked being able to see her family. She told him she loved seeing all her extended family and she loved the house, and that it was so close to her mom, that it made it just perfect. She thanked Jacob and gave him a big hug and kiss, and told him she loved him very much.

He ask her if she still wanted that forth child, and she gave him a grin and said what do you think? Jacob ask her, what if we have more than one again this time? She told him that would be great if they did, that she woud love them just the way she does the triplets.

Jacob ask her when she wanted to start trying again, and she winked and grinned at him, and said how about tonight? He gave her a hug and said wait until I get you home then darling.

The plane landed about fifteen minutes later, and they all headed home. Jacob held Lainie's hand in the car all the way home, and she just smiled.

When Cheryl helped her get the kids ready for bed, she told her that she and Jacob were going to try to have more kids. Cheryl hugged her and said "good luck". I will always be here to help you with all the babies you have.

That night after her shower, and she got into bed, Jacob took her in his arms, and they made love biggest part of the night. Lainie just couldn't seem to get enough of Jacob. After they both fell asleep in each other arms, they slept like babies. Next morning, whey they woke up, Jacob told her he wanted to make love to her again. It was still to early for the tripets to be awake, so they made love for the next hour or so.

Jacob told her he wanted to make love to her every night and every morning, to make sure she would get pregnant again. Of course, she agreed, because she wanted more kids, and was anxious to get pregnant again.

She had gone off her birth control pill about two weeks before that. She thought it might take a while for her to conceive again, and she wasn't taking any chances that she might not get pregnant again so soon.

For a month, Jacob made love to her every night and then again in the morning . When it came time for her menstrual cycle, days went past and it never came, so she was excited and couldn't wait to tell Jacob. So that evening she ask Cheryl if she would mind watching the kids while she and Jacob went out for a while. Cheryl told her she would be more than happy to watch them.

When she and Jacob went to the restaurant, she waited until they had there meal on the table, then she told him she had something she had to tell him. He just smiled and said, I know what you are going to tell me. You are pregnant aren't you darling? She told him she was, and ask how he knew. He told her he had been taking note of when her period was suppose to have been, and he knew she was late. He took her in his arms and hugged and kissed her, and told her she had made him the happiest man in the world again.

Everyone in the restaurant was looking at them so Jacob said, we are going to have a baby.. The whole restaurant started clapping and congratulating them.

When they got home, Jacob made love to Lainie again that night and first thing the next morning. He told her even though she was already pregnant, he was going to keep on trying. She told him to never stop making love to her. He said, "you never have to worry about that", I will always want to love you darling.

This time she had no morning sickness, and at three months, she was already showing, and had to wear maternity clothes. She was hoping that she would have more than one again this time. She dearly loved the three she already had, and knew she had love enough for lots more.

Her doctor told her that being pregnant really agreed with her, and that she was doing well. He told her they would do an ultrasound in another month or two. He didn't want to say anything at this time, but he thought she might be in for multiple births again this time, He thought he heard more than one heart beat when he examined her. He wanted to wait until he did the ultrasound to make sure, and right now, it was a little early to be real sure.

The two months past really fast, and at five months along, the doctor did the ultrasound. When he had the wand on her stomach he immediately heard, one, two, three heartbeats. At five months, she looked like she was ready to deliver. The doctor ask Lainie and Jacob how they would feel about three more babies all at once.

They both said that was wonderful, they ask if the doctor could tell if they were boys or girls. The doctor moved the wand around again and saw there was one girl and two boys this time.

She was so excited , and so was Jacob. He said this is what we wanted again was more than one. The doctor told Lainie to take it easy, but she could still do what she wanted for right now.

As the months past, Ethan, Emily and Ellie were all excited about the new babies. They wanted them to hurry up and get here. The helped with the nursery and picking out clothes for them. Of course, there was still the baby clothes that that they had worn, and they wanted to new babies to wear them too.

The babies were born a month early, and they were all under four pounds, but were all healthy. The boys they named Alex and Aaron, and the little girl they named Aleese.

They were kept in the hospital for two weeks so they could gain some weight before they were released. They grew fast though, and soon they were going home.

Leslie, Jason and the girls came out to see the new babies after they came home, but Jay had to work and couldn't get the time off to come with them, besides, he had a girlfriend he didn't want to be away from either.

Laura and Lane held and fed the babies. They didn't want to go back home when Jason and Leslie was ready to go, they wanted to stay and help with the new babies and to help with Ethan, Emily and Ellie.

Lainie loved having Laura and Lane there and they were so much help. She hated to see the time they would have to go home. Time flew by so fast and all the children were growing so fast. Cheryl told Lainie she wanted to go to Ian's cabin for a few days, and since Laura and Lane wanted to stay to help with the kids, that she would take this time to go for a few days.

She left the next morning for the cabin. When she got there, she felt as if Ian were there with her. She went for a walk down to the stream. She sat down on a rock, and stared at the water.

When she got back to the cabin, she climbed up to the loft. There she found boxes containing all of Lainie's clothes. She started going through them and thought maybe Lainie would like to have them, so she loaded them in her car. She found a doll Lainie had played with and put that in her car to.

She stayed for two days at the cabin, and then went back home. She told Lainie that she had brought back all her old clothes that were at the cabin. When she went through them, she found the shorts and tops she had on the day Ian had taken her from the park.

She said, I remember that day as if it were yesterday. I missed my mom, but knew I couldn't go back home to her. I am so sorry Ian had to die, he was a great father to me, and

I loved him very much. I did find my mom after Ian told me where to call and I also found my brother and sisters who can share my life with me.

Seems like things have turned out the best they could, but I do wish Ian was still here with us too. I know he is looking down from Heaven and sees all of us here. Cheryl, thank you for making his last years very happy. You always seemed like a mother to me, and always will.